The

Courtship

The Cosmic Courtship

By Julian Hawthorn

Published by Cirsova Publishing™

The Cosmic Courtship first serialized in All-Story Weekly, Vol 78 1-4 (November 24, 1917, December 1, 1917, December 8, 1917, and December 15, 1917).

First Pocket Paperback Edition: 2021

ISBN-13: 978-1-949313-50-5

About the Team

Michael Tierney not only made his pulp library available for this project, he provided the photographic images of these rare magazines so that a manuscript could be produced. He has also lent his years of experience digitally restoring damaged pulp art to restore the original cover by Fred W. Small to create a unique cover for this edition.

In 1972, around the time he was editor of his high school paper and a State Finalist in Journalism, Michael Tierney's first tale of the *Wild Stars* appeared in the fan pages of *Eerie* magazine.

By the age of 22 he was managing a printing division of *International Graphics* and released his self-published magazine; *The Multiversal Scribe.*

Now an elected City Councilman, he has been a bookseller for nearly 40 years and finalist for multiple retailer awards. An *Overstreet Comic Book Price Guide* advisor since 1999, he has written over a thousand industry articles and reviews.

Cirsova Magazine published five of his short stories, including *Shark Fighter*, his posthumous collaboration with Edgar Rice Burroughs on *Tarzan and the Mysterious She*, and most recently serialized *Wild Stars 5: The Artomique Paradigm.*

Cirsova Publishing released a 35th Anniversary set of his four previous *Wild Stars* novels, and a *Wild Stars Omnibus.*

Chenault & Gray released his four-volume *Edgar Rice Burroughs 100 Year Art Chronology* in 2018, and his *Robert E. Howard Art Chronology* is coming soon.

Beyond the Farthest Star, a weekly online comic strip that he scripts, colors, and letters, began in 2019.

Troll Lords released his *Wild Stars Role Playing Game* in 2020.

His work can be found at: www.thewildstars.com

Robert Allen Lupton has painstakingly recreated the text as it was originally published from the digital images provided from Michael's collection.

Robert is retired and lives in New Mexico where he is a commercial hot air balloon pilot. Robert runs and writes every day, but not necessarily in that order. More than a hundred and seventy of his short stories have been published in several anthologies including the New York Times best seller, "Chicken Soup For the Soul—Running For Good". His novel, "Foxborn," was published in April 2017 and the sequel, "Dragonborn," in June 2018. His first collection, "Running Into Trouble," was published in October 2017. His next collection, "Through a Wine Glass Darkly," was released in June 2019. His newest collection,

"Strong Spirits," was released on June 1, 2020.

His third novel, "Dejanna of the Double Star," was published in December 2020.

His edited anthology, "Feral: It Takes a Forest to Raise a Child," was published September 1, 2020.

Robert has been an active Edgar Rice Burroughs historian, researcher, and writer since the 1970s. His contributor page on the ERBzine website is: https://www.erbzine.com/lupton/, and includes several of his articles and stories.

Follow Robert on Facebook and see over 1000 drabbles, his 100 word short stories based on Edgar Rice Burroughs, at:

https://www.facebook.com/profile.php?id=100022680383572

P. Alexander compared the text produced from the scans against the originals to ensure accuracy of this edition to the work as it was first published in All-Story Weekly. He is the editor of Cirsova Publishing.

For more information: www.cirsova.wordpress.com

Additional Titles from Cirsova Publishing

Michael Tierney's Wild Stars®
I: The Book of Circles (2019)
II: Force Majeure (2019)
III: Time Warmageddon (2019)
IV: Wild Star Rising (2019)
Wild Stars 35th Anniversary Omnibus (2019)

Jim Breyfogle's Tales of the Mongoose and Meerkat
Vol I: Pursuit Without Asking (2020)
Vol II: The Heat of the Chase (Coming in 2022)
Vol III: TBA

Other Works
Duel Visions, by Misha Burnett and Louise Sorensen (2019)
Endless Summer, by Misha Burnett (2020)
The Paths of Cormanor, by Jim Breyfogle (Coming in 2021)

Table of Contents

CHAPTER I
MIRIAM'S VISITOR

THE twenty-second of June, of the year 2001, was Miriam Mayne's birthday—her twenty-first. She and her father, Terence Mayne, the billionaire contractor, had arranged to meet at the Long Island house for dinner. After an early breakfast, she kissed him good-by; he went down-town to business, and she to her room, to put on her traveling dress.

A glorious day it was! When the tall girl stepped from the window of her room on to the balcony, the sun embraced her graceful figure as if it loved her; the perfume of flowers rose up like incense; two humming-birds, busy with the morning-glories, buzzed a welcome; the air was warm but exhilarating. She mounted to the wide parapet of the balcony and stood poised for a moment before starting on her journey.

She was clad in a dove-colored suit of a tunic and trousers to the knee, fitting snugly, but allowing freedom of movement. On her feet she wore a pair of sandals, with appendages on the heel resembling the talaria of Greek myth, ascribed to Iris and Mercury; but for the wings were substituted triangular projections of a pliable metal with a silvery sheen. Over her head was drawn a close-fitting cap, fastened securely under the chin, and bearing wing-like excrescences similar to the foot-gear. A wide belt or girdle encircled her waist; it was formed of narrow vertical pieces connected together, and four buttons or small knobs appeared on the front of it, where they could be readily reached by either hand. In her right hand she carried a light staff.

The art of personal flight was still a novelty at this period, though the principle of it had been known for several years. Only persons of sound physical and mental coordinations were apt to attempt it. Miriam had not only passed the government tests, but was considered an expert.

With an upward swing of the arms, she leaped into the air; the drop to the pavement of the court below was some fifty feet; but she rose upward as if she had no weight, and continued her ascent until she hovered at a height of a couple of thousand feet above the far-extending city of New York. There she paused, gazing hither and thither at the magnificent prospect.

From the Battery to Harlem, the surface of Manhattan Island was covered with handsome villas and mansions, of white or tinted marble, standing each in an ample enclosure of green turf studded with trees and flower-beds. Several miles to the south rose the superb turreted pile of the new Madison Square Garden, like a fairy palace, of white marble set off with pinnacles and trimmings of gold. It was Terence Mayne's crowning achievement, and was still unfinished. The East and North Rivers were spanned by between three and four hundred bridges, lofty and wide, made of a metallic substance that glittered and shone in the sun. The beds of the rivers themselves were laid with white concrete, over which the water flowed blue and transparent. Northward, beyond the island, the city proper stretched for forty miles, following the course of the Hudson, but extending westward over a breadth of five miles into New Jersey; the home of nearly fifteen millions of people. From side to side, and from end to end, no smoke fouled the clear air, and no sign of factories or of business traffic was visible. But the entire area had been excavated to a depth of a thousand feet, and here, layer beneath layer, were housed the business activities of the metropolis.

Miriam was not unfamiliar with these subterranean regions. Illuminated by the electron light, and ventilated by the carbon process, and kept at an even temperature of seventy degrees Fahrenheit, they were wholesome and pleasant, and many thousands of the inhabitants never troubled themselves to appear above-ground from year's end to year's end. Except for the absence of sun, moon and stars, life in this artificial world was as agreeable and convenient as on the surface. But sun, moon and stars, and the fathomless depths of space, were indispensable to Miriam's happiness.

She now pointed her staff eastward, and began to move gently in that direction. She was using the ten-mile-an-hour stop in her belt; she had no present need for haste. She flew, leaning forward on the air, at an inclination of about twenty degrees from the vertical, without movement of her limbs. Few individual fliers were abroad, and they passed at a distance. But three of the great Atlantic liners were setting their course east and southeast; and high overhead, flocks of buses carrying business men were sliding swiftly toward the lower part of the city. In spite of its external transformation, New York, in some human respects, had not changed much in the last hundred years.

In crossing the Sound, a sea-gull flew past Miriam, and she, by a sudden turn, swept so close by it that she was almost able to touch its wing. It dodged and dived with a scream. Smiling to herself, she gave a supple impulse to her body, which caused her to slant slightly downward across the Sound toward the Long Island shore. Five hundred feet above the ground she resumed a horizontal course, moving slowly across the green lawns and parklike enclosures that surrounded the sumptuous county-seats of this district. It was a fair sight; but the sun, now forty-five degrees above the sea-line, dazzled her eyes; she turned her body with a leisurely and luxurious motion until she lay with her face toward the western sky, where a snowy flock of gossamer fine-weather clouds was strung across the blue. She was now carried along as if reclining on a couch, and did not change her posture until she heard the rhythm of the surf on the great eastern beaches. Fetching herself upright again, she touched the gravitation-control in her belt, and sank slowly, guiding herself with her staff toward the left. In a few minutes she alighted buoyantly on the soft turf of the great Mayne estate.

Fifty yards before her rose a grassy mound, with a sort of summer-house on its summit; the place was protected by a grove of tall pines, disposed in a wide semicircle between the dwelling-house and the ocean. Entering the pavilion, she quickly threw off her flying-suit, and running down the steps to the beach, she plunged into the surf. So was Artemis, in the seclusion of her temple precincts, wont to bathe on the Lydian shore of the Ægean. Heading out beyond the breakers, Miriam swam and dived and splashed up diamond spray in the thrilling coolness. At length she came ashore, borne on the crest of a white-maned steed of the sea, and ran back, a virgin shaft of glistening whiteness, to the pavilion. Thence, after an interval, she reissued, robed in a flowing gown of purple wool, lined with orange silk. She seated herself on a curved bench of marble that stood on the seaward crest of the knoll, and spread out her black hair, thick and long, to dry in the sun. Seated thus at ease, and secure from all disturbance, Miriam fell into a reverie, which gradually became profound. The intense but restricted sphere of personal consciousness closed itself in the broad, steady luminousness of perception which comprises and permeates the individual as does the ocean its waves. The beautiful capacities of nature became transparent.

A voice of agreeable quality was speaking to her "Miriam!" The call had been repeated several times before she recognized her own name. No one was within sight or hearing. She knew the methods by which, in late times, science had overcome space for both ear and eye; but this voice was using a method unknown to her.

"Hold yourself still," it now said, "and you will see me."

She imposed quiescence upon mind and body. A shadow flickered for a moment before her, and vanished. It came again, less vague. Upon the empty air between herself and the sea it gradually defined itself. A tall, grave figure in a dark robe with a black silk cap on its head. The face was pale, with large, black eyes under level brows, it expressed tranquility and power. As she gazed, a blue star surrounded by a ring glimmered forth over the figure's left breast. The lips moved, and the quiet voice spoke again.

"I have observed you for a year. We are companions of the star. We can help each other. Will you meet me?"

"What star?" asked Miriam, though she did not speak aloud.

"Saturn! The desire of your heart may be accomplished. I have found the way, but can go no further without you. Will you meet me?"

The eyes of the apparition, meeting hers gravely and almost sternly, communicated confidence. The speaker was a woman.

"I am willing!" said Miriam after a long look.

The expression of the face softened.

"You will receive a letter to-morrow. I have taken this method that you might act freely. Without sympathy there could be no—" The voice died away; the figure dimmed and a quivering passed through the air-drawn scene. The next moment, nothing was visible but the sun-steeped sea and shore.

Miriam stayed where she was for a long time. The influence had not been hypnotic, but had conveyed a strong sense of spiritual harmony and of enlightenment. She recognized the value of spontaneity. Knowledge was not acquisition, but revelation. Her visitor had understood her need.

Miriam was a woman of her time. After acquiring political equality with man, the other sex had soon turned from political activities to science. Her more finely organized and fresher brain and her spiritual intuition opened to her realms of conquest over nature and methods of achieving it hitherto unimagined. The revolutionary investigations and discoveries of later years had been woman's work. Etheric heat, planetary motive-power, electron light were gifts from woman's hand. She had divined the parallelism between material fact and spiritual truth. A lever so powerful began to make the rock of human ignorance stir in its bed. The birthday of the universal man seemed near.

To Miriam, keeping abreast of progress, had come some time since the dram of actual interplanetary communication, not by interchange of signals merely, but by bodily transference from the earth to other worlds of our system. She had never confided this ambition to any person, and her fantom visitor had been the first to divine it—for such had seemed to be her intimation. Her father, a man of a past age, never suspected it. All the girl's studies had had this ambition for their end, but hitherto her progress had seemed small. But to-day for the first time she could feel, with a tremulous joy, that her labor and self-discipline had fitted her for what was to come. A powerful hand had grasped hers and a profound and fearless intelligence would direct her course. It was an added joy to know that her cooperation was needed even for her guide's masterful intelligence.

The personal equation had begun to be recognized as the most important agency of man's rule over nature. It found its analogy in the inter-atomic force. By solving the true nature of the isolation which the personal equation implies, the way to its mastery was found to lie in the compensating attraction of innate sympathies. Proper use of this vital truth could result in achievements otherwise unattainable and seemingly miraculous.

Miriam's mother, a lovely and intelligent woman, had died when the girl was fifteen; her father, though a man of the old fashion, was in his way a genius, of immense energy and ability; and the whole tide of his ardent Celtic nature flowed into love for his daughter. He had the insight to perceive that she must allowed great freedom of choice and action in order to secure her best development; he let her make her own rules of conduct and education, and merely supplied whatever means and facilities she required; there was complete mutual love and confidence between them. She came and went, studied and played, as she pleased, without supervision or question; and as she grew up the visible results were fully satisfactory. Her bodily strength and symmetry were united with supple grace; she was trained in the great gymnasiums which the influence of the king had made fashionable; she was expert in fencing, swimming, running and wrestling; and, besides her aptness in flying, was a consummate horsewoman. Terence Mayne never learned personal flight, and hardly liked to have his girl "mix herself up with a lot of ducks and geese," as he put it; but he was always eager and proud to act as her cavalier on a ride, and they were often seen cantering down the Long Drive side by side, he with his bushy gray hair uncovered to the breeze, thumping up and down on his big hunter; she undulating easily beside him on her fine-limbed Arab. The vision of her beauty haunted the dreams of many an impassioned youth. But Miriam, though always kind and frank, drew back from male intimacies. She was wedded to science and desired no human husband. Her father forbore to urge her.

"A pretty gal is a good thing; let 'em stay so long as they will. The woman in 'em will have her say in the long run; don't let us be meddling!" This was his rejoinder to the suggestions of sympathetic friends.

On her side, she recognized his cordial and sociable temperament, and never refused her cooperation in his great dinners and receptions—a queenlike presence, with her black hair and sea-gray eyes, moving through the glowing vistas of the great rooms. Side by side with her intellectual proclivities, there was in her a deep emotional quality, which found expression in forms of art, and which she used to give distinction to the plans and details of her father's social enterprises.

But the greater part of her time was devoted to thoughts and effort far removed from such matters; these had for her a sort of sanctity, due to their exalted character. Science, in that age, had a spiritual soul which lifted it toward the religious level. The solution of her problems was connected with the future of mankind; it required courage to face even the prevision of them. Transcendent moments visited her, mingled with a sentiment of profound personal humility. She was conscious at times of an appalling loneliness, chilling her to the finger-tips with delicious terrors. But anon the warm blood flowed back to her heart, and she would rise and pace her chamber, crowned with the hope of being forever known and blessed as the giver to her race of unimagined benefits.

Her spectral interview on the Long Island estate brought a new influence to her.

The next morning at breakfast she found the most commonplace-looking letter imaginable beside her plate. The contents were as follows:

DEAR MIRIAM:

My laboratory is at Seven Hundred and Ninety-Sixth Street, near the river. Come at three o'clock any day. Pardon the abrupt way I presented myself yesterday. It was made possible by our saturnian affiliations. I am still a little awkward about it—the interruption was caused by an accident to the coordination. I hope to fulfil your expectations. I am myself more than ever convinced that we shall achieve together something that will modify the course of human history.

Sincerely yours,

MARY FAUST.

Miriam looked across at her father, who was immersed in his business mail. How near and dear to her he was, and yet how far removed! Distance is but the relation of one mind to another; we may be closer to the Pleiades than to the companion whose arm is linked in our own. But diameters of sidereal systems cannot sever us from those we love.

She said nothing to her father; but that afternoon she privately visited Mme. Faust's laboratory; and thus began a secret connection destined to have important issues.

CHAPTER II
RACE FOR LOVE

A LITTLE more than a year after Miriam became Mary Faust's pupil and partner, the new Madison Square Garden was opened with the annual horse-show, which, for ages, had been a leading function of New York society.

The new building covered four city blocks, and was raised above the vast plaza in the midst of which it stood by flights of ornamental steps. The great central tower rose fifteen hundred feet above the pavement, and the towers of less elevation stood at the four corners. Forests of delicate columns supported the superstructure, which mounted height above height in snowy elevations, finely touched with gold and color, till the central tower leaped aloft like a fountain. So just were the proportions of the whole that the edifice seemed rather to rise upward with an aspiring impulse than to press upon the earth.

The populace filled the plaza, thronged the steps, and streamed inward through twenty broad doorways. The king and court were to attend the ceremony of the opening, and the uniforms of the guards divided with their bright lines the masses of the crowd. Air-boats, like great birds, chased one another high overhead in sweeping circles, dropping small parachutes carrying bags of sugar plums, which were caught by the crowd. The October sun shone on the front of the marble edifice, kindling all into airy splendor.

A young man of modest demeanor but of striking aspect was slowly edging his way through the throng. He was nobody in particular—an artist, Jack Paladin by name. But he was tall, well formed and handsome; his fellow students in the art class, a few years before, found a strong resemblance between him and the statue of Hermes, ascribed to Praxiteles, and used to get him to pose for them. Jack was good-natured and easy-going; but his mind was not centered upon himself. It did not even dwell upon one or another beautiful girl, with whom he could imagine himself in love. He thought of and loved nothing but art: was a *Galahad* of art, in short. Mankind and the universe were to him material for pictures: his constant problem and delight was to make them serve art purposes. He had little money, and only one living relative—his uncle, Sam Paladin, quite a notable personage, who had been a great traveler and adventurer in all parts of the world, a hero of daring escapades, a soldier of fortune; but now, at a little less than fifty, had settled in New York, enjoying the society of a few old friends and applying himself enthusiastically to astronomy; as if, having exhausted the resources of this planet, he were seeking further entertainment in other satellites of our sun. Jack had no heartier backer and sympathizer than Uncle Sam, though art was an unknown region to him. Though by no means a rich man, Uncle Sam devised all sorts of pretexts for "tipping" him; and Jack was obliged to stipulate that his uncle was not to buy any picture of him which had not already been sought by some outside purchaser. Hitherto, the outside purchaser had seldom brought the stipulation to the test.

Jack was going to the horse-show because, if anything could share a place in his heart with art, it was fine horses. He had almost been born on horseback, and there were few better riders alive. Since horses had been retired from utilitarian service, the art of breeding had been cultivated, and magnificent animals were produced.

As he reached the broad flight of steps at the front of the building, bugles announced the approach of the royal party. The king and queen, simple and unostentatious persons, drove up in a carriage-and-four of the fashion of fifty years ago. The popularity of the monarch was attested by the cordial greetings of the populace. The old man's stately head was uncovered, and he bowed with kindly smiles at the acclaim. On the platform at the top of the steps a group of officials awaited him, foremost among them Terence Mayne, with a tall black-haired woman by his side. Jack happened to get himself within arm's reach of this woman; she slowly turned her head, and their eyes met.

At first her smooth cheeks paled; then she lowered her eyes, and her face was covered with a blush. At the same moment the music of ten thousand silver bells sounded; the royal party reached their hosts and changes of position occurred in the group, so that the black-haired girl disappeared. But her image had entered Jack's soul and banished all else except the purpose to follow her forever!

Availing himself, unobtrusively, of his great strength, he made his way to the interior immediately in the wake of the royalties.

The spectacle was astonishing—an oval of blue and gold nine hundred feet in diameter surrounding the dark red tan-bark of the arena. From above the seats, which accommodated one hundred thousand spectators, arches rose to the spring of the tower, meeting at the base of the golden dome, through whose central aperture further heights were visible, with frostwork arabesques, ascending into a misty vagueness of rainbow light. The royal box was in the center of the middle circle of seats, and to the left of it Jack soon identified the gray hair and stalwart figure of Terence Mayne chatting with the Maharaja of Lucknow. But the girl of his soul was nowhere to be seen.

"Miriam Mayne is to ride in the ninth race, I hear," said some one to some one else at his elbow. Miriam! That must be she! How he worshipped the name!

At another bugle-blast, several hundred beautiful animals entered the ring and began to move round it. Many of the riders were women. The usual riding-costume for both sexes was a close-fitting silken tunic and leggings: the hair of the women flowed loose from a fillet, or hung in braids. As the procession passed him Jack noted in the ninth rank a rider on a white Arab. Dense black hair streamed out from beneath her fillet; the movements of her body were full of supple dignity, replying to those of her horse; she rode without saddle or bridle; her dress was gray silk embroidered with gold, and in her right hand she carried a red rose. Miriam!

Jack leaned far over the balustrade. Miriam Mayne, in the magic of a moment, had thrown wide the gates of his heart and transformed the boy dreamer into the lover full grown. She was blood to his heart and air to his lungs. To be hers—to make her his!

As she drew near she did not look toward him; but her Arab began to curvet and dance, and she playfully struck him on his glossy neck with the rose. Hereupon the beautiful creature reared erect; she flung her body forward, and in the act the rose somehow escaped from her hand and fell into Jack's breast. She passed on.

Had she meant it? Jack dared not believe so. He had never considered the effect upon a woman of his commanding stature and noble bearing. Many a fair woman had followed him with her eyes, in vain.

But here was her rose, the most sacred object he had ever possessed! Did it not create some ineffable understanding between them?

The parade filed out, and on consulting the program Jack found that Miriam's race was two hours hence. He determined to visit the stalls below.

Among the noticeable horses was a roan, belonging to the maharaja, seventeen hands, to be ridden in the ninth race by a Mohammedan groom as big as Jack himself. Jack took a fancy to him, and, though warned by the groom, entered his stall and petted him. He was a natural horse-tamer. After a few moments the formidable creature responded to his advances, and the groom stared.

When he returned to the arena the royal party had withdrawn and the spectators, freed from court etiquette, were visiting one another and strolling about the lobbies. But Miriam was nowhere to be seen. However, as he was ascending the tower on one of the escalators, he saw, through the carved interstices, a party descending on the opposite side. An exclamation broke from him.

She was there, with her father and the maharaja. Her back was toward Jack. But as they passed she turned slowly, and for the second time their eyes met. Oh, the poignant delight to him of that moment! As she averted her glance she seemed to notice the rose in his doublet, and he thought she smiled. The next moment the relentless machinery of the escalators had separated them and hope of overtaking her was vain.

Returning to the arena he found Miriam absent from her father's box; the latter was talking animatedly with the prince, and near by stood the big Mohammedan groom with a dejected air. It seemed that he had just stabbed another attendant and was under arrest. The official was sorry, but an assault with a deadly weapon could not be overlooked. As no one else could ride the roan, the animal must be withdrawn from the race. The maharaja smiled and bowed politely, shrugged his shoulders, and resigned himself to the will of Allah; but gave the groom a glance that boded no good for his near future.

Jack had an inspiration; he flung a leg over the railing of the box and strode up to its astonished occupants. "I'll ride for you," he said to the maharaja, "I know your horse and can manage him."

His highness gazed at him with an inscrutable Oriental smile. Mayne, his Celtic temper already somewhat ruffled, growled out in the brogue that always more pronounced in emotional junctures, "An' who might *you* be, me frien'? Ye have yer nerve wid ye, anyhow!"

Before Jack could reply a long-legged, athletic figure came striding down the aisle with a grin of amusement on his aquiline features. It was Uncle Sam!

"It's all right, Terence!" he called out, a laugh in his deep voice. "That's only my nephew, Jack. How do, prince? Oh, the boy can ride, all right. If you want to win that race, the youngster can come nearer doing the trick for you than any other jockey on the track!"

The atmosphere changed. None ventured to dispute Sam Paladin. Terence smoothed his hostile front. The maharaja bowed with engaging grace. "My horse has killed six men," he observed in liquid tones, "but I see your nephew is a big, brave man. I am content—Bismillah!"

Jack lifted his head and his chest expanded; his eyes shone with joy. "Thanks, uncle; thanks, prince!" he said. "I'll fix it!" and he was off. He remembered afterward that he ought to have said something nice to Miriam's father; but it was too late.

There was a bare twenty minutes before the ninth race. Jack, the pacific, plunging down to the basement, abruptly became the despot of the stables. He stripped the roan of the cumbrous saddle, patted him, divested himself of shoes and doublet, bound the broad blue sash of the maharaja round his waist, fastened Miriam's rose over his heart, vaulted at a bound astride the great horse, and was ready for the ring five minutes ahead of the bell.

Some of the best horses and riders in the world faced the starter—seven of them. The champions of England and of Australia; a black from Morocco, carrying a Berber prince as black as he; a famous Chinese mare bestridden by a mandarin's daughter; a wiry brute from Russia backed by a Cossack. But where was Miriam?

Jack's heart sank. Without her his presence was a farce. True, honor bound him to defeat her if he could; but he believed her Arab was unbeatable. The riders took their places, while a murmur of admiration from tens of thousands of lips created a soft but thunderous vibration in the enclosed space. The starter's arm was uplifted!

"Miriam, my soul, where art thou?" Had Jack spoken aloud? At all events, as if in response to a summons, and to Jack's unspeakable delight and agitation, out she paced, quietly, from behind the barrier and moved to a place directly at his side!

She gave no sign, however, of recognizing his presence. She tossed back over her shoulder a heavy strand of her hair, leaned forward and whispered in her stallion's ear, then straightened her limbs and lifted her body, alert with life and vigor. At the second signal she crouched forward over the withers and threw up one arm, keen for the signal. It came—the race was on!

Jack, with a hoarse shout of love and war, made himself one creature with the roan, and they hurled forward. His blood thundered in his veins, the frenzy of his pulse was answered by the leap of his steed. They flew forward smoothly, and the ground swept beneath them like the fleeting of a cataract. Hippomenes and Atalanta—a memory of that, read in a shadowy corner of his father's library, sped through Jack's mind.

Triumphant power, mingled with the exquisite sense of Miriam's companionship, made him greater than himself. He knew, without looking, that she was still at his side, riding with elastic ease. What a girl! What a rider! What a queen of heart and soul, whom he with heart and soul was striving to overcome!

The first circuit was a free course; after that, obstacle succeeded obstacle, each of increasing difficulty. Few would survive the finish! The great ring seemed to speed round like the rush of a whirlpool. The riders were trying out one another's powers. As yet there was little change in their relative positions. With the first obstacle, foresight and strategy began to match themselves against mere swiftness.

Jack suddenly felt that Miriam had changed her place, but at the jump a waft of her hair touched his cheek and something like a great white bird swept past him; she alighted just ahead of him, closely followed by the mandarin's daughter on her gray. The two girls had outmaneuvered him.

Rapid vicissitudes followed. At the third fence the Englishman collided in mid air with the Berber and both came down in a headlong ruin. As Jack swung into the fourth circuit a tall, white fence with a ditch beyond it rose before him; some one was at his shoulder; but Miriam and the Chinese girl had already passed it. The roan leaped a thought too soon, and his hind feet failed to reach the edge of the ditch; in regaining it he was passed by the Cossack, with the Australian at his heels. Jack was last in the race!

But the roan was fresh as ever, and two circuits of the course remained. Jack, moreover, knew by a sixth sense that he and Miriam would finish together, with the rest nowhere. A glimpse of Miriam flashed before him, leading the field by a scant head, her hair streaming out like a sable oriflamme to lead him on. Like a bolt shot by Hercules, the roan answered his call. The Cossack and the hardy Australian fell to the rear, but Jack and the former swung around the corner nearly abreast; the two girls were close in front; all four would take the final jump almost together!

The spectators were on their feet and the air roared with the gigantic diapason of their cheers. Jack's nerves were steady as iron now and his spirit dilated, till the whole desperate struggle seemed to be taking place within himself, and the end foreordained.

The last barrier was seven feet high, at the top of a slight incline. Beyond was a six-hundred yard stretch to the tape.

The mandarin's daughter, riding superbly, but near the end of her physical endurance, had the gray's head at Miriam's knee. Miriam, at the incline, slightly abated her pace; the other shot forward at full stride, but her mount, embarrassed by the incline, struck and snapped the top rail and fell, with the near foreleg broken on the further side. Miriam, in leaping, had to swerve to escape the sharp end of the broken rail and to avoid landing on her rival. But the latter picked herself up unhurt; the gray lay kicking on its side.

Meanwhile the Cossack, relying on the lightness of his horse, took the incline at top speed, grazing the roan's shoulder as he went by, and he and Miriam, in unison, but on converging lines, rose in the air. With Jack between them, a catastrophe was imminent. A hush, followed by hissing of breath drawn between the teeth, showed that the spectators realized the peril.

Jack, self-possessed in that crisis, knew what to do and had the power to do it.

Miriam's white Arab cleared the bar first and unscathed; but the kicking gray beneath caused him to stumble on alighting and he fell on his right side. Miriam threw her right leg over his head as he fell and thus avoided injury, but she was unseated and thrown heavily; unprotected from the Cossack and from the hoofs of the struggling gray, she lay prostrate, partly stunned.

The Cossack leaped ruthlessly; but Jack leaped with him, at an angle which hurled the Russian aside; the fence crashed and fell, the man pitched on his shoulder, breaking his collar-bone; his horse, recovering, scurried riderless down the course.

Jack, descending, saw beneath him the pale, upturned face of Miriam, her eyes half closed. To all in the house her instant death seemed inevitable; in the horror-stricken interval shrieked out the voice of old Terence Mayne: "My girl! My girl!"

But as the roan with stiffened forelegs dropped earthward, Jack flung himself far down on the left, holding on by arm and heel, Indian fashion; and before those deadly hoofs touched the tan-bark, he gathered up the unconscious girl with his right arm, regained his seat by an incredible effort, and thundered on to the finish with Miriam across the roan's withers.

A long-drawn roar of amazement and relief greeted them. Even in that age of unmatched horsemanship, such a feat had never before been witnessed. The roan was halted; Mayne, Sam Paladin and the maharaja were pressing through the throng. Jack slid to earth with the girl he loved still in his arm; and thanked God, humbly, in his heart.

CHAPTER III
LOST!

TWO days after the horse-show opening Jack stood in front of an easel, in the studio on the top floor of an up-town building. He had charcoaled on the canvas a design of a girl on a horse. No model for either figure was in sight; but the artist's rapt expression suggested that his eyes were opened to things invisible to common senses. The girl had long, black hair, and the horse seemed to be a white Arab stallion.

The only other person in the big, empty room was an undersized boy of fifteen, who was short one leg. He had the aspect of a clever and good-natured gnome. He was occupied in cleaning paint-brushes and was whistling softly to himself.

A soft, bell-like sound, thrice repeated, suddenly proceeded from a small black box affixed to the wall. The artist, roused from his vision, frowned.

"Say I'm busy, Jim," he muttered. "Only ten o'clock, too!"

Jim hobbled to the box and shot back a panel, disclosing a mirror six inches square, in which appeared a miniature but lively image of a middle-aged man of athletic build and aquiline features. "It's yer Uncle Sam, boss," he said.

Jack sighed, laid down his palette, and strode over to the box.

"Good morning, uncle," he said, addressing the image. "What's up?"

"Get over here at once—very important—quick car!" the other replied, with an urgent gesture.

"Would this afternoon do, uncle? I'm awfully busy just now—"

"Don't lose a moment!" rejoined his uncle, beckoning imperiously. "That girl of Mayne's, you know—the old man is in a devil of a taking—come on!"

Jack's bearing changed, as if a million volts had passed through him.

"In five minutes, uncle!" he exclaimed, slamming back the panel. "Stay here till I call, Jim," he added to the gnome.

"Right! Here's yer tile, boss," the latter returned, extending a hat to his master.

"Cut it out!" exclaimed Jack, pushing it aside, with no realization of what it was. He stepped on the lift in a recess of the wall and vanished upward like a clay pigeon from the trap. Emerging on the roof, he seated himself in the little air-boat stationed there, cast off the moorings, seized the wheel, set the needle, and had the craft skimming southwestward like a bullet. In four minutes he had traversed the twelve miles to his uncle's house and found Sam Paladin awaiting him on the landing. While Jack was gasping out, "What has happened to her?" the elder man cast an amused glance at the boy's costume—an old velvet jacket, out at the elbows and daubed with paint, knee breeches of the same period and condition, red slippers and hair on end. "Come below and I'll tell you," he said. "Too bad to take you away from your work!"

Jack, following his uncle to his rooms, uttered inarticulate sounds and trod upon the other's heels. The seasoned adventurer pushed him into a chair, sat down opposite him, handed the cigars, took and lit one himself.

"Ordinarily," he observed, "I'd be the last person to interrupt a man in his professional business; but this thing is a bit out of the common. Terence and I are old pals, and he has a notion fixed in that obstinate noddle of his that you are the man for this job. The way you picked up that girl at the show gave him a high conception of your general ability. I must confess I don't see how you managed it! I guess your back muscles must be in good shape. If you can repeat the trick—not in just the same way, to be sure—you might consider your fortune made. Terence, as you probably know, has all sorts of money, and would think nothing of tipping you a million or so, if you made good."

"Uncle—please! Is she hurt?" What—"

"What are you breaking that cigar in pieces for? Was it a bad one? Take another!"

"Uncle, I—"

"Oh, well, here's the story. To-day is Wednesday. The show was on Monday. Terence says all went as usual on Tuesday, up to six o'clock, afternoon. At that hour the maharaja was to dine at his house tête-à-tête—no one else but Miriam—that's her name I believe. I have a suspicion that the maharaja is rather hit by the young lady. And the prospect of becoming Rani of Lucknow might appeal to her—but that's another matter!"

"Miriam marry that damned heathen!" shouted Jack, standing up and raising his clenched fists. He could not get out another word, but his red face, blazing eyes, and rumpled hair were eloquent and formidable.

"I don't know about the prince's religion," said Uncle Sam calmly; "but he's a good enough fellow: was educated at Oxford: has a fine palace at Lucknow—I stayed with him there, once, for a fortnight. But all that is aside from our present business. It seems Terence had made it a point with Miriam to be present at this dinner, and she had promised; he says she never failed to keep an appointment in her life. He got home from his office at four o'clock Tuesday: Miriam not in: she was in the habit, he believed (but he always left her to do what she liked) of being absent most afternoons, and sometimes till late in the evening. By five-thirty he was dressed for dinner; Miriam had not returned. At six sharp the maharaja arrived; no Miriam. They waited for her an hour: no signs of her or message from her. Maharaja very polite, but serious: Terence—well, you can imagine his state by this time, and how pleasantly the dinner went off. Nine o'clock—no news! The prince took leave, still very polite, but— Terence, sending out searchers in all directions, and taking rapid leave of his senses. Sleepless night: morning: No Miriam! No trace or vestige of her. Terence called me up at nine-thirty: had a revelation from Heaven that you are the man in the world who can find her: insisted on my taking up the matter with you at once. Now, of course, the girl may be nothing to you; but it's my opinion that if you could find her, and were not immutably set against matrimony, you'd stand a good chance against his highness. So here we are!"

While Jack was devouring this recital with one part of his mind, another was recalling an episode in his career which had taken place within the past thirty-six hours. In the first place, there had been a tremendous, palpitating minute or two, after the rescue, when he had had an opportunity to speak to Miriam in private. In that minute he had desperately dared to tell her that he loved her, that heaven and earth could not keep him from her, and had implored her with the most impetuous and irresistible adjurations to grant him an interview the next day. The girl, under the influence of these words and of the general situation, had finally replied that if he would be at a certain spot at a certain hour the following afternoon, he might have his wish. The rendezvous was, in fact, in the avenue bordering the high wall which enclosed Mary Faust's grounds and laboratory. Suffice it that the tryst was kept; and from two o'clock until near three things were said by the two young people to each other, which, considering that both of them had been, until that time, vowed to celibacy and to science and art, were sufficiently remarkable and important. Miriam had also briefly indicated her relations with Mary Faust, and her habit of daily study there. The lovers parted in delicious agitation and happiness. And it now appeared, from his uncle's chronology, that Jack was the last person, except Mary Faust, to whom Miriam had appeared in the flesh. The last, that is, unless she had left the laboratory for the dinner at home, and had been lost on the way. Either she was with Mary Faust at this moment, or she was lost—probably kidnaped. Jack had the immense advantage over all other searchers of the possession of this clue. As to the kidnaping hypothesis, he refused to entertain so intolerable an idea, at least until he had proved that it was not Mary Faust!

Lovers are at once the most outspoken and the most secret persons in the world. It might have seemed natural that Jack should confide his story to his uncle, his only intimate friend. He did nothing of the kind—the matter was too sacred. At the conclusion of Sam Paladin's statement, the young man adopted a reserved demeanor, intimated, vaguely, that he happened to be in possession of some facts which might lead to something, promised to undertake the task at once, and to communicate promptly whatever news he might obtain, and forthwith rather hurriedly excused himself. Five minutes later he was back in his studio, and with Jim's expert assistance was preparing himself for the adventure. At a little after eleven, the two stood before the door of the Faust laboratory.

Sam Paladin, meanwhile, after a half-hour's meditation, during which he sometimes smiled and sometimes looked grave, transferred himself to Mayne's habitation, and went into private session with that distracted personage.

"The boy is in love with the girl," he told him, "and love is the best sleuth in the world. He knows something—wouldn't say what—he is on edge, body and soul, and whatever is humanly possible, he will do to find her. Of course, your girl may not care for him; but if she does, the problem will be the easier. It wouldn't surprise me if we got a message before evening. Some accident has occurred, no doubt; but there's no reason to suppose it serious. In these times of occult researches very funny things sometimes happen; but they commonly turn out all right. If I thought otherwise, I should advise you to get drunk. As it is, take a cold shower and a nap."

"Naps and cold showers for a father whose daughter is maybe murdered this minute!" moaned Terence, whose appearance emphasized his words. "If that lad of yours brings her back to me safe and sound, he may take all I've got—except the girl! I'm ready to start in again carrying bricks up a ladder, as I did thirty years ago; but the girl is the girl; there's none like her; and if I had the solar system in me pocket, I'd not swap her for it—once I got her in me arms again. 'Occult,' d'ye say? 'Funny things!' If ever I get me hands on the parties that's handed me this deal, believe me, I'll occult 'em, and funny won't be the word for their feelin's, neither."

"If you hand over your property to Jack, I've no doubt he'd let you board and lodge with him and his wife," remarked Sam Paladin composedly. "But this is all foolishness. You'll hear from Jack before dinner time, and good news, too!"

"Dinner time? That's seven hours off, and how will I kape living till then?" demanded Terence, taking his head between his hands and planting his elbows on his knees, like the effigies of despair in Dante's *Inferno*. "Ye'll find the cruiskeen lawn in the cupboard, Sam, lad; take what ye want, but stand by me till the end," he added after a while, looking up from the depths of his misery. "No, none for me!—though never did I think to see the day when Terence Mayne would turn his back on whisky! Wurra, wurra!"

"Try a draw of the pipe, anyway," suggested, Sam; "I see the end of it sticking out of your pocket. Here's tobacco," he said, proffering his pouch.

"The plug is better," replied Terence, proceeding slowly to fill a blackened old clay from the loose chippings in his pocket. He then drew a match along his thigh and lit up. "A bit of old times!" he sighed; and as the two friends puffed fragrant clouds at each other, the lines of anguish on the Irishman's visage were softened.

CHAPTER IV
MARY FAUST

"HERE is where I saw Miss Mayne last," said Jack, as he and Jim paused before a massive door studded with iron nails, in the western end of a high cement wall, on which the shadows of the trees bordering the avenue were thrown by the noon sun. "It's just twenty-one hours since that door opened, and she went in."

"What opened it, boss?" inquired the gnome. "I don't see no handle."

Jack thought a minute. "She pressed her thumb on one of those nails," he said. "I think it was this one," and he laid a finger on the third nail from the west edge of the door, four feet down from the top. Jim examined the nail carefully.

"Guess yer right, boss," he muttered. "That ain't no real nail, it's the top of a spring. Will I try a punch on it?"

"Wait!" said Jack, arresting his hand. "As I remember, she pressed it in a particular way—like this!" He pressed the nail-head, which yielded to the impulse; then twice again, in rapid succession; then a fourth punch after a moment's interval. The door swung heavily inward, and the two companions stepped quickly within. They found themselves in a spacious garden, planted with flowers and ornamental bushes; a path led up to a house made of gray stone, with an iron dome thirty feet in diameter projecting from its roof. Jim, after a glance around, shut the door behind them, and hobbled after Jack, who was advancing up the path. In a few moments they reached a doorway on the east side of the building, at the top of a short flight of steps. Jack laid a hand on the latch, which yielded, and the two entered. They passed down a corridor, which brought them to a stairway. Up the stairs they went, Jim's crutch tapping on each step as they ascended. The stair wound upward for a considerable distance; at length they emerged on the landing, and saw another door, with a heavy blue curtain hanging before it. As Jack stepped toward it, it was pushed aside from within, and a tall figure in a dark robe stood before them.

"Who are you? What do you want?" asked the figure. The voice, quiet and deep, was evidently a woman's. The face, pale, with regular features and level, dark brows, might almost have been a man's, such was the power and firmness of its expression.

Jack's eyes met hers intently. He was sending the whole force of his nature into the gaze, and she was conscious of it; they measured each other.

"Jack Paladin—a friend of Miriam Mayne's," he said after a moment. "I parted from her at your door yesterday afternoon—you are Mme. Faust, I suppose? She has not been seen since. Her father sent me here. Is she here?"

"Does her father think she is here?"

"I alone know she comes here," answered the young man.

"Who is this?" inquired the other, indicating Jim, who was scrutinizing her with great interest.

"My trusty servant," returned Jack.

"The gen'leman saved me life, lady," put in Jim. "Catch'd me in his arms, fallin' out of an air-boat. I bumped him good, and bruk me leg; an' I'd go to hell and back for him, any time, surest thing you know. That's me!"

"His is not the only life you have saved, I understand," said Mary Faust, continuing to fix her eyes on Jack's face. He blushed red. "I am come for Miriam Mayne," was his rejoinder.

She was silent for some time, seeming to take counsel with herself.

"Come with me," she finally said, and turning, held back the curtain that concealed the room beyond. Jack entered, Jim following; and she brought up the rear. The room was large, with a high ceiling, which was pierced by the shaft of a great sidereal telescope mounted beneath it on massive piers which passed through the floor and were no doubt anchored in the ground far below. A wide table, covered with diagrams and other papers stood in a window on the north. Several machines of odd construction were disposed here and there. Of these, the most noticeable was a structure of black metal, shaped somewhat like a large chair or throne; the seat-room was cushioned with blue silk; at the right side a hand-lever projected, connected with a powerful system of geared wheels; in front was a funnel-like projection formed of copper wire coiled in a spiral, the diameter of the cone diminishing outward. On the sides of the structure were clock-like disks, the hands pointing to astronomical signs. Above the chair was suspended a large hollow hemisphere, highly polished, and covered with flowing designs somewhat resembling Persian writing. The chair was placed facing a broad open window opposite the eastern sky. The whole contrivance may have weighed more than a ton, and, like the telescope, rested on solid foundations passing through the floor.

Jack gave all this a passing glance. He had no head for mechanics. Jim, on the contrary, had a natural insight into machinery, and he examined this strange object with a fascinated but perplexed expression.

"I have doubted how best to make known what has happened here," said Mary Faust, "but your coming has forced me to a course which is, perhaps, the best. Miriam Mayne was here on Tuesday afternoon—has been in the habit of coming here for more than a year past, as my pupil and assistant. Together we built this engine. It is psycho-physical; its function is to transport persons from this earth to other planets of the solar system. But it was not to be used until means had been perfected for their return hither."

"Gee! dat's big stuff! How does yer work it, lady?" required Jim.

"I shall explain it when Miriam's father arrives—I have already sent for him," said she, addressing herself to Jack. "Meanwhile, if your nerves are steady, I will show you something. But bear in mind that appearance misleads; sleep resemble death, and trance still more. The spirit has no relation to space."

Jack drew in a long breath; his heart was beating painfully. He felt as if he stood on the brink of a fathomless abyss, from the depths of which things unimagined were to arise. The woman took his hand and led him to a large cabinet on the left. Her touch sent through him a strong vibration, which seemed to calm his mind and fortify his resolution. The cabinet had folding doors; she touched the knob, and they opened wide. The interior was lined with blue satin, and was illuminated with a white light. The figure of a young woman lay there, apparently deep asleep. Her hair flowed beside her like a black river. On her left breast glimmered faintly a blue star: it flickered like a flame.

At the sight, Jack stiffened and trembled. His grasp tightened upon Mary Faust's hand. The serene, cool pressure of her fingers steadied him. "Miriam—here!" he uttered in a husky whisper.

"A part of her," rejoined Mary Faust quietly. "The garment she wears on this earth. Miriam is absent. The flickering of that star is the assurance that she lives."

"Where is she, then?" demanded Jack, with dry lips.

"She is on the planet Saturn," replied Mary Faust.

CHAPTER V
"I'M GOING"

THESE astounding words were so composedly and confidently spoken as to make incredulity clash against conviction in a bewildering battle. Jack's knees relaxed, and there was a prickly sensation over his scalp.

"Sattum!" muttered Jim. "Must be in Jersey. I never heard of it—not me!"

"Things more startling have become commonplace by use," remarked the woman. She was about to say more, but the entrance of Terence Mayne, accompanied by Sam Paladin, interrupted her. She closed the cabinet and moved forward to receive them.

The father was too much agitated and exhausted to express himself conventionally; but the appeal of his eyes was poignant and pathetic. Sam Paladin, as always, was master of himself, and he greeted Mary Faust with urbane courtesy.

"I am this boy's uncle; I ventured to accompany my friend Mayne on the chance that I might be of use. I hope you have good news of the young lady?"

"Your daughter is alive and well," said Mary Faust, turning to Mayne. "But she is gone on a long journey. I would have notified you at once, but delayed in the hope of being able to fix the time of her return. That however is still uncertain."

"Some little accident, I understand?" said Sam cheerfully.

"I will outline what took place," she replied. "This machine combines material with spiritual forces in a way not hitherto attempted. It separates these components in man, and directs the immaterial part to any point selected; the physical body remains here, entranced, pending the reunion. Other planets of our system may thus be visited at will."

Mayne probably understood nothing of this. Sam had followed her keenly.

"I've been something of a traveler myself," he remarked, "and after bringing my explorations on this globe to an end, I adventured, through my telescope, into other fields. I had looked forward to a time when we might communicate intelligently with our planetary neighbors, but there is novelty in your plan. But supposing you to have arrived at your destination, divested of your mortal body, how would you make yourself manifest in a practical way to the mortal people out there?"

"A natural law, of which I am the discoverer, covers that difficulty," the scientist answered. "The spirit of an inhabitant of any earth, on reaching another, is spontaneously clothed with a body proper to that globe, and, of course, endowed with its language. This has long been known to me; but only recently, and with your daughter's assistance," she added to Mayne, "have we succeeded in effecting actual transference from one to another."

"How far away is my little gal gone, ma'am?" demanded Mayne, in a faltering voice.

"Whether the distance covered be a mile or millions of miles, the principle is the same, and the distance is unimportant," she replied. "The planet Saturn, where she is now a guest, is between eight and nine hundred million miles from where we stand."

Mayne dropped into a chair with a groan, and even Paladin arched his eyebrows. Jim, for whom such figures had no significance, was busy investigating the parts of the machine. Jack had sunk into a profound meditation, and was perhaps as remote from the circle as Miriam herself. His uncle was the first to speak.

"From what you say, I infer that Miss Mayne's physical part is here?" he suggested.

"What happened is this," she returned. "After Miriam's arrival here yesterday, I was in another room for several minutes to fetch some materials. When I returned, I found her sitting in this chair, unconscious. The pointer indicated Saturn. She must have seated herself, and inadvertently pressed the lever. I signaled Saturn and learned of her safe arrival there; but neither I nor they had prepared means for her return. Since then I have been occupied with this problem."

"Then—?" interjected Sam.

"I have made this explanation in order to prepare Mr. Mayne for what he is to see," observed Mary Faust. "Do not attempt to touch her; she is protected by forces whose disturbance might involve grave consequences both for you and her."

She moved to the cabinet, followed by the two elder men; Jack remained in his revery.

When the doors were opened, Mayne, with a faint cry, staggered toward the sleeping figure, but Paladin restrained him. The starlike light upon the girl's breast, flickered as before; at long intervals a slight movement was perceptible in the chest and diaphragm, as she drew her breath.

"Respiration in Saturn is slower than with us," Mary Faust remarked.

"What is the cause of that bluish light?" Sam inquired.

"It is the Saturnian sign," she replied. "It indicates the connection between the spirit and its body here."

"Don't deceive me, woman—is she alive?" burst out Mayne, hoarsely. He was trembling like a man shaken with palsy.

"Be assured of that!" was her grave answer. "On the spiritual plane, what we call distance is but difference in mental states. Miriam is now temporarily in the Saturnian phase. Her return will be as an awakening from slumber."

"Waken her, then!" cried the old man, passionately. "Mother of God, is there no way of undoing your devil's work?"

Jack had drawn near the others, and now laid a hand on Mayne's shoulder.

"Don't be discouraged, Mr. Mayne," he said quietly. "I'm going after her, and I'll bring her back."

This announcement, which the speaker's countenance emphasized with a look of serious resolve as unbending as natural law, caused all present, including Mary Faust, to hold their breath for a moment. Then the croaking voice of Jim broke the silence.

"Dat's de right stuff, boss! an' I'm wid ye!"

CHAPTER VI
THE LEVER

A GREAT resolve is magnetic: it transforms the bystanders. Jack, modest and shy by nature, suddenly became the leading personage of the group. He had not spoken rashly or without realizing what his purpose involved. A journey of near nine hundred million miles, and back again, across the void of space! Courage, faith, devotion, consciousness of resources adequate to cope with the unknown, belief that love, the moving power of the universe, was more than a match for all obstacles—these were his armor and weapons. He would follow Miriam, find her, and bring her back! The youth assumed, with the words he had uttered, the stature of a hero; and the hearts of his hearers bowed before him.

His uncle, in whose blood the hero strain was still warm, looked in the boy's eyes and stifled the remonstrance that sprang to his lips. It was an enterprise in which any man might have been proud to perish. Old Terence Mayne stared at him speechless: then, tottering forward, leaned his gray head upon Jack's shoulder and sobbed aloud. Finally, Mary Faust stepped up to him and took both his hands in hers.

"All power that is mine I give to you," she said. "You are worthy of the adventure. You are worthy of her you seek. You will find her: more, I cannot promise. But you do not need more. The will of God be done!" She drew his head down and kissed him on the lips. It was the accolade of the new-made knight.

Before taking his place on the machine, Jack stood for several minutes looking down upon the form of Miriam, as if to draw into himself, through the medium of that beautiful image, the perfume of the spirit he was to pursue.

He turned at length, his face cheerful and tranquil. He exchanged a mighty grip with his uncle. To Mayne he said, as the latter grasped his other hand: "When you see us again, sir, she will be my affianced wife."

"I love her more than life and all," replied the old man stoutly; "but when I see her yours, I'll love her more yet!"

Mary Faust now threw about his neck a gold chain with a pointing hand attached to it, wrought out of a sapphire. "It is the mariner's compass of your voyage," she said.

'Good-by, Jim," said Jack, enclosing the little gnome's fingers in his large clutch. "Take care of Uncle Sam while I'm away. Did you finish cleaning the paint brushes?"

"Sure I done 'em, boss" answered the boy, in a piping tone, his black eyes sparkling like diamonds. "Good luck and happy days to yer!"

Jack stepped on the throne; as he did so, the hollow hemisphere above his head glowed like molten metal, and zigzag flashes played to and fro within it. An undertone of deep sound vibrated through the room. Jack, with a farewell glance at the others, laid his right hand upon the lever.

As he was about to press it down, Jim, who had crept round to the left, made a sudden spring with his crutch and landed across his knees. The lever descended, and they were off!

CHAPTER VII
800,000,000 MILES

"NOT a bit what I expected," murmured Jack to himself: "not the least!"

He looked around him, turning slowly this way and that. On every side stretched out a plain—if it were a plain; but it had no horizons—no curvature. In fact, though solid beneath the feet, it was not easily distinguishable from the medium in which he stood, moved and breathed. It was transparent, too, in all directions, below as well as above and sidewise. It was as if he were walking on water—or in water, like a fish. This medium, however, had a luminousness of its own: not sunlight or moonlight, though sunlight itself was not so bright and clear. Moreover, yonder was what looked like the sun—probably was the sun, indeed; it shone like a white fire, and had no shadowed side, like the other spherical objects that floated at various distances round about it, and which he now surmised must be planets. Yes, planets of the solar system, evidently; and that large one, somewhat below and to the right was our own earth; the masses of north and south America, and part of western Europe, were recognizable, lying lustrous on the dark oceans; and there was the moon, just clear of it on the further side; they must be very far off—several hundred thousand miles. Jupiter—that must be Jupiter, with the belts and the red spot—looked much larger than the earth, although more remote. Jack must have been traveling at a good pace during the few minutes since pushing down that lever in Mme. Faust's laboratory—if it were a few minutes, and not a few days or years: there was no way of telling. Was he stationary now, or still moving? That too was not easily decided.

Jupiter?—where then was Saturn? His heart began to beat hard; was he on the way? He gazed before, behind, to right and left; nothing that looked like Saturn appeared. Not below him, either. Above, perhaps? Ah, yes, there it was! It hung directly in his zenith, a lovely vision, the ring clearly defined all round it; its hue was a delicate sapphire, not the yellowish tinge that earth's atmosphere gives it. It was very distant; its apparent size had increased hardly at all. And yet, as Jack gazed at it, it seemed suddenly to grow larger, as if it had been projected directly toward him. But that could not be; rather, he had moved at an inconceivable speed toward it. This was strange!

At this juncture he was acutely surprised to hear a voice—a human voice, a familiar voice, none other than Jim's, in fact, addressing him in these words: "Slow down a bit, boss: Gee, dat was a dandy jump you made! I ain't got me sea-leg yet: slow down!"

Jack turned toward the apparent source of this appeal, but at first could see nothing of his attendant, whose existence he had quite forgotten. Presently he discerned a dot in the pathless void, immeasurably remote: could that be Jim? He narrowed his eyes, and now became aware of a new peculiarity in his environment: Jim, though still in seeming size no bigger than a flea, became distinctly visible in his minutest details; nay, he could even hear the tap of his crutch as he exerted himself to bridge the gulf between them. The mere act of attention—a mental process—could have the effect of abolishing space to the senses!

"But the boy can never come that distance in a dozen years!" he murmured half aloud.

"Try anudder t'ink, boss," replied Jim's voice, close to his ear; "Watch me!"

While these words were uttering the flea enlarged to the dimensions of a bee, and was still coming. What was it that Mary Faust had said about space? "A difference in mental states?" In other words, thought, on the mental plane was presence!

As he meditated this discover, understanding began to flow in upon his mind from various quarters, like the light of dawn through crevices in a darkened room. He had left his material body on the earth; he was now all mind—spirit, though he could perceive no change in his outward aspect; his garments seemed the same; he was substantial as before; though there was no air in space, he breathed and his heart beat as usual; though space was absolute cold his body had the warmth of summer; though there was no blue sky, the etheric light—if it were that—was intense as the electric flash and iridescent as the rainbow. Upon distant objects it had the effect of a lens of enormous power.

"I'm what is called dead," said Jack to himself, summing up his ideas. "This is my spirit—my me itself. I'm not dead for good though—my body down there is only asleep. To travel is to pass through a series of thoughts in continuous succession with a fixed end always in view. I once read, 'As a man thinks, so is he.' To be in Saturn, I must think myself into a Saturn state of mind. Just how to do that isn't clear; but I'll see what wishing myself there will do; wishes may be wings!"

"Dat sort o' dope is beyond me, boss," said Jim; "but if hangin' on to your coattails is any good, count me in!" Jim had arrived.

"You're not scared, are you, Jim?" said Jack, smiling down on him.

"Nix on scared!" was the reply. "I al'ays t'ought it would be a fine t'ing getting out o' N'York; but I never t'ought t'would be like this!"

Jack now applied himself to concentrating his mind on his destination, which he figured as Miriam, with a sapphire halo round her head. They were moving through the solid, yet diaphanous medium at a speed which could be estimated only in planetary terms; but with no sense of bodily exertion. All at once Jim cried out:

"Hully Gee! will yer lamp dat, boss!"

Jack looked: the spectacle sent a shock through him, as when one suddenly sees the red glare of an express train bearing close down upon him. A vast red disk covered twenty degrees of the eastern firmament. The planet Jupiter stood revealed in all its details. Raging whirlpools of fiery storms tore its surface, diversified with dark streamings and appalling abysses. Jack fancied he could feel the terrific heat radiating from it; flames hundreds of miles long licked out toward him.

Accompanying this paralyzing sight was an awful humming sound, and a feeling as of being drawn into the vortex of an inconceivable red-hot maelstrom. The gigantic disk seemed nearer!

"The sapphire hand!" spoke the quiet voice of Mary Faust, like a whisper in his ear. Had she been observing his progress from her station on the other side of the diameter of the solar system?

He had forgotten the talisman that was to guide him across space: he grasped it, and in the same moment felt the rush past him of an invisible tide of forces; as, when one is being swept down the headlong torrent of a flood, he catches at some stable object, and the wild waters tear at him as they hurtle past. The sapphire hand barely stemmed the rush. As Jack hung there, in doubt whether he were saved or doomed, he seemed to see wild figures racing past him, snatching at him as they flew; fierce, beautiful faces convulsed with passion; contorted bodies of giants; the flaring out of fiery hair like streamers of the northern lights. They gnashed their teeth, the glare of their eyes was as the flashing of torches. But the sapphire hand was cool in his own, and its power prevailed.

"Dere was never no subway rush to beat dat!" was the manner in which Jim expressed his feelings, as the tension abated.

A powerful arm was thrown across Jack's shoulders, drawing him out into freedom, and a voice like the tones of a mighty harp exclaimed laughingly:

"Those Jovian fellows are always on the lookout to catch people napping. They must be disciplined. If you hadn't thought of your compass when you did, I should have had quite a struggle getting you free. You are from Faust, are you not?"

Jack nodded; he was panting from his exertions. Then he looked at his new friend.

A superb being he was, quite as tall as Jack, and with a body so beautifully formed that the earth-man, a connoisseur in such matters, could not restrain a cry of admiration; so might the god Apollo have disclosed himself in vision to the sculptor who vainly strove to reproduce him in the Belvedere. He glowed as with an inner light; his features seemed divinity incarnate; his hair, thick and waving, of a golden hue, flowed down upon his Olympian shoulders. There was no excess of muscular development in trunk or limbs, but irresistible power declared itself in every contour and movement. "Who are you?" Jack asked.

"I am called Solarion," the other replied; "I am stationed in the midway here, to look after travelers from your earth, who are specially liable to kidnaping by these Jovians, who make serfs of them. But, you," he added, scrutinizing Jack more closely, "belong to a new type: I have only met one other—a girl, bound for Saturn. Our friend Mary Faust has been preparing the route for some while past; but it was not thought that she had yet completed her arrangements. A wise woman, that!"

"You met a girl—who was she?" demanded Jack with devouring eagerness.

"Miriam was her name—a lovely child— Ah, I see! you have come after her! Well, you must expect difficulties; it is much easier to make the trip out than to get back again. The Saturn folks are very agreeable people;

but you two are such an attractive pair that I fear they may want to keep you." He laughed good-humoredly as he spoke, sending a very keen look into Jack's eyes. "It's taking a risk, you know," he added. "I would help you if I could, but my domain is restricted to these outlying regions. I am assuming, of course, that you and she—or either of you—will care to return. Saturn is a pleasant country."

"Little old N'York is good enough fer us, mister, and don' you fergit it!" put in Jim earnestly. "We was jest takin' a look aroun', dat's all!"

Solarion smiled amusedly. "You'll have a good story to tell your friends," he observed. "Few of them will have traveled so far on one leg."

"My boss figgers we'se sperrits," said Jim; "sperrits is angels, ain't dey? Wot I want to know is, is dere any odder angels wid one fin off, like me?"

"You are only partly a spirit as yet, Jim," answered Solarion, patting the urchin's head. "When you cut loose altogether, you will find your leg in its place again."

During this colloquy, a stupendous distance had been traversed; Jupiter was now but of the apparent size of our moon; and Jack had latterly been conscious of a new influence, gentle and soothing, accompanied by warbling sounds resembling those of an æolian harp, which waxed and waned upon the ear. The dazzling whiteness of the medium surrounding them had become modified, and now took on a faint violet tinge. A delicate perfume, too, like that of wild flowers, but with a peculiar aromatic quality pervading it, was perceptible.

"Do I imagine these things, or are they real?" he asked his guide.

"Look!" was the reply.

As he spoke, the position of all three underwent an alteration. Hitherto they had been moving continually in the same course relative to the station of the earth and sun, but now they insensibly turned, as an arrow turns in the air after completing its outward flight. Immediately in front of them rose a mighty arch, with another arch defining itself above the first, and parallel with it. A minute more, and the first arch had become a complete circle, with the other surrounding it. The color of the interior sphere was a royal purple; the outer ring flashed with prismatic hues of enchanting splendor. Scattered here and there in the void around this apparition were five or six much smaller globes, each of a different tint—red, blue, yellow, green, golden and silvery. The voyagers were dropping swiftly down into the midst of this marvelous earth. It expanded until its circumference covered the entire field of sight; rivers, mountains, forests and plains were now discernible. A few breaths more, and they would alight there!

In the awe and wonder of this revelation, one thought and emotion filled Jack's soul: Miriam! As the downward rush continued, Solarion laid a hand gently on his head; his senses swooned, a tender darkness closed his eyes; the shouting of a myriad voices seemed to vibrate in his ears for a moment, and was then hushed; and he knew nothing.

CHAPTER VIII
THE RED SPIDER

JACK was lying on his back on the ground. In the beautiful sky overhead hung what looked like a vast silvery simitar, the curved edge downward, flashing in the sun, if it were not itself the source of light. The weapon extended its arc from horizon to horizon: beautiful but menacing, it was suspended over him like a cosmic sword of Damocles, and without any visible support: were it to descend, it would not only cut Jack in twain, but the planet on which he lay, and any others of our system which might lie in its path.

Jack's attention was especially drawn, however, to a red, globular object, at a great but incalculable height above him, and near the arch of the simitar. It had the appearance to his eyes, which were still somewhat dazed by recent events, of a huge red spider, with hostile designs upon his welfare. As he stared at it, unable to move from his position, the spider detached a scarlet thread from its body, with a tiny globule at the end of it. It swung to and fro in immense curves, and constantly lengthened its radius: it was dropping toward him with inconceivable rapidity. The globule at the end of it now assumed the aspect of a living creature or monster of some sort, clewed up there like an acrobat in an aerial flight. Nearer and nearer it came: the swinging movement of the thread to which it was attached had nearly ceased, and it was descending straight downward. In another minute the acrobatic monster would reach the ground.

It plainly behoved Jack to stand on his guard. He was convinced that the apparition meditated no good to himself. What he had done to provoke it he could imagine as little as he knew what it was, or where in the universe this event was taking place. But the proximity of danger stimulated his faculties, and by an effort of will he summoned together all his energies. He lifted himself to a sitting posture, and in another instant he was on his feet. At the same time memory, and control of his nerves, sprang into action. He remembered his flight through space: he must have landed on Saturn: and here he was, having as yet hardly drawn his first Saturnian breath, confronted by an adversary who apparently intended to prevent his drawing many more!

The red object now hung a few feet above the surface of the ground, and not more than fifty paces from where he stood. It was a sort of vehicle of hemispherical form, and out of it leaped a being in human shape, with red mantle twisted about his body, shaggy black hair, and a dark and frowning countenance. In his right hand he grasped a short truncheon. He advanced straight upon Jack, who, wholly unarmed, put himself in an attitude of defense. If it came to fist fighting or wrestling, he thought he might stand a chance, though his antagonist was a man of superb proportions and physical development. But Jack had a well-grounded confidence in his ability to tackle any man on equal terms, and to give a good account of himself. In many athletic trials and combats he had never yet met his match; and unless his present opponent took some unfair advantage, he saw no reason for doubting that he could put up a fight worth seeing.

At five paces distance, the man in the red mantle halted and addressed him.

"I will give you your choice," he said in a deep voice, "of either becoming my slave or dying where you stand. I hold here"—he shook his truncheon threateningly—"the means of blasting you to fragments in a moment. I am Torpeon, Prince of Tor. Kneel down and do me homage!"

Jack was somewhat relieved to find that the Prince of Tor spoke American, or what seemed to be that famous language, though he afterward found reason to think that special conditions may have misled him on that point. An underlying sense of humor in him was also awakened by the grandiloquent terms in which this remarkable person launched his challenge: they reminded him of the defiance of medieval champions that he had read about in books of romance. Being aware of no ground of enmity between them, he thought it proper to make a statement on his own account.

"I am Jack Paladin of New York," he said. "I've just landed here, and I'm not acquainted with any inhabitant of this planet, and therefore can have no quarrel with any. I came here in search of a young lady, a friend and countrywoman of my own, who arrived here a few days ago. When I find her, I intend to take her back to New York. I'm not looking for trouble, and I guess you have made a mistake in your man."

This placable speech, instead of soothing, had the effect or rousing the other to even greater wrath. His features assumed a terrible expression.

"Silence! or take the consequences," he growled raising his truncheon. "The woman you speak of, Miriam, is in my power: and I shall take her with me to Tor and make her my wife. Once more I give you the choice of either serving her and me as our slave, or of perishing on this spot. Kneel!"

But the Prince's allusion to Miriam had put Jack into another humor. He became very grave and punctilious.

"You are evidently a footpad of some sort, and I shall have pleasure, if you insist upon it, in breaking your back across my knee. I'll take my chances against your revolver, or whatever you call that thing in your hand: if you were not a coward and a rascal, you would throw it down and meet me with bare hands, like a gentleman. What you say about the lady is a lie, and if you don't take it back immediately, of your own motion, I will give you the most unpleasant quarter of an hour of your life in making you swallow it. Now, then, if you're ready, I am!"

The prince grinned a dreadful smile, and pointed his weapon at Jack's head. The latter kept an eye fixed upon the hand that held it, prepared to dodge and make a spring for him at the proper moment.

In that moment of suspense he heard the quiet voice of Mary Faust speaking.

"The sapphire talisman will protect you from his lightnings," she said. "Put forth your strength, and do your best!"

"Thanks: I will!" was the reply flashed back by his mind. He knew that she would hear him across the gulf of space, as he had heard her. Meanwhile, though he had been prepared for the worst, he felt decidedly encouraged by the information about the truncheon.

"Here is your end, then," said Torpeon between his teeth.

As he spoke, a red flash issued from the end of the truncheon, which was leveled with true aim at Jack's forehead. The result was surprising to the Prince, and highly agreeable to his antagonist.

The lightning bolt-bolt, if such it were, swerved from its course at an inch or so from its mark, and slipped round Jack's head as a jet of water would be deflected round a glass sphere. The ozone whose scent hung in the air had a reviving effect rather than otherwise. Torpeon, himself, unbalanced by the shock of astonishment, did not have opportunity for a second attempt. Jack had made his spring, catching the right wrist with his left hand. He gave it a violent wrench, causing the truncheon to drop from his grasp. The weight of Jack's impact against Torpeon's body caused the latter to give ground, and the two men came to earth together, Jack uppermost.

Now began a struggle of heroic dimensions. Jack was not long in becoming aware that the strength he had to contend against surpassed anything heretofore experienced. Torpeon was a giant in power, and was fighting with a fury and desperation more than tigerlike. Had he been as well trained as was Jack in the science of wrestling, in the grips and shifts which bring leverage to bear against muscle, in the surprises and swift changes of that ancient and noble art, Jack would have had a labor of Hercules indeed. But that practised skill was lacking: Torpeon secure in his magical resources, had never been at the pains to prepare himself for personal struggle.

The grip of his great arms round Jack's ribs was a sensation to be remembered. Jack's right arm had also been caught in the vise, but his left was free, and he applied pressure beneath the other's bearded chin, forcing his head back slowly and surely, until the imminence of a broken neck compelled the other to relax his hold. With both arms now liberated, the champion of America, twisting his body like a serpent, got a knee under Torpeon's right elbow, and bore down upon the right forearm with a weight and power that caused agony almost unendurable: and foam flew from the prince's lips. At the last extremity, however, he got his other arm round Jack's neck, and using it as a fulcrum, tore himself free and staggered to his feet. But he was panting hard, and his right arm hung temporarily useless at his side. Jack was also well-breathed, but in much the better shape of the two. He had also fought himself into a good humor, and was disposed to friendly parley.

"There's good material in you, if you'd taught yourself how to handle it properly," he said. "I'm a peaceable sort, and I don't want to hurt you. I have other things to attend to besides thrashing princes: and if you're willing, I'll call this thing off, and we'll both go about our business. Or, if you're not satisfied, I'll try you out at sparring. But you'll have to look out for my left uppercut."

Torpeon, out of the corner of his eye, had caught sight of his truncheon lying on the ground near by, and thought that if he could repossess himself of it, he could make good the miss of the first discharge. He had felt enough of the stamina of his adversary to prefer whatever advantage he could command: and he was edging toward the weapon in the hope of getting a chance to pick it up, covering his design with words.

"You are a valiant warrior," he said, compelling his features to assume an amicable aspect. "I need men like you at my right hand in the government of my kingdom. With you to help me, we can conquer the inhabitants of this planet, who are pusillanimous and averse from battle, and become rulers of all the globes that surround the sun."

"It's a handsome offer," replied Jack smiling; "but I was never addicted to the business of ruling. The best thing you can do is run back home and take a thorough course in athletics; and then, if you ever happen along our way, I shall take pleasure in showing you over New York, and, if you like, I'll take you on either at boxing or wrestling for points before the Royal Referee in the Madison Square Garden arena. We hold an amateur meet every year. But first, if you please," he added, in another tone, "I'll trouble you to take back what you said about a certain lady. You were lying, were you not?"

He made a step forward as he spoke. Torpeon, however, had by this time got close enough to the truncheon to feel safe in making an effort for it. He made a leap backward, at the same time stooping to snatch it up. But neither of the combatants, preoccupied with each other, had noticed the advent of a third party, who was now revealed.

Taking advantage of the cover afforded by bushes and rocky projections, this individual had gradually crawled nearer and nearer, until he was now as close to the fallen truncheon as Torpeon himself. He anticipated Torpeon's movement by the fraction of a second, and seizing the weapon, he rose to his feet, and presented it at the prince's breast.

"Han's up, now, or I'll blow de guts out of yer!" he cried out. "I hol's de winnin' ace, and de boss an' me, we scoops de pot. Han's up!"

Torpeon stared in amazement. His new antagonist, grotesque, one-legged and dwarfish, appeared to have sprouted out of the ground. He was supernatural: and he had him covered with a steady hand. The odds were too great.

"Drop that thing, Jim!" called out Jack. "We don't need any machinery to tackle this hound: what he wants is a kick!"

So saying, and incensed at the prince's attempted treachery, Jack stepped forward with a foot prepared, as on the gridiron of former days, for execution. But Torpeon's red chariot still hung close at hand at the end of its long thread. He made a spring for it, caught it by the rim, and swung himself aboard. Immediately the cord began to diminish its length, carrying the chariot up with it at a prodigious speed; in a few minutes it had become a mere dot in the sky, ascending toward the red spider which the prince had called his kingdom of Tor, and which, as Jack, with cleared faculties, now recognized, was one of the ten moons which accompany the great Saturnian world on its endless journey.

"Well, he's gone home, and I think he'll stay there for the present," said Jack, with justifiable satisfaction. "If he'd been properly brought up, though, he'd have made a good center rush on the team."

"Dat guy is no good for nottin', believe me, boss," said Jim. "He ain't got de right sperrit: he's not a game sport! Dis here gun of his is a bum model: I makes a bluff wid it, but I ain't on to her workin's. I wisht I'd busted him wid her, anyhow!"

"Better as it is," Jack said. "So you landed here safe and sound! Have you any notion whereabouts we are, or which way we should go to find Miss Miriam?"

"Yer kin search me, boss. Say, is dat big white t'ing up dere all right? I'd not like to be roun' when it's her day fur droppin' down!"

"That is Saturn's ring, Jim," replied Jack wearing his new-found wisdom lightly. "It's perfectly safe: I could have shown it to you through uncle's telescope any time."

"Well, N'York was never like dis," said Jim, dissatisfiedly. "I likes to see plenty of folks aroun', and here ain't nobody 'cept you an' me an' de guy what you give de hidin' to: Say, boss, you polish him off great! Ef you'd landed on his jaw, he'd be takin' de count yet! Me, I was rootin' fur yer all de time!"

Jack nodded appreciatively, and then cast a glance over the landscape.

It was level and interminable: the horizon as distant as if from the top of a mountain: the arc of the ring passed out of sight beneath it on either hand. There were tracts of forest, the windings of a mighty river, expanding here and there into gleaming lakes: in another direction a chain of mountains sparkling as if formed of crystal. Flowers grew everywhere, and the color on all sides was almost as bright as if objects emitted rather than reflected light. But no sign of human life was visible: this planet, many times the size of our earth seemed to be unchanged from its primeval state.

"Robinson Crusoe thought he was lonely on his desert island," muttered Jack. "What would he have said to a desert world! Eight hundred million miles from home, and not so much as a red Indian in sight! And my darling girl abandoned in such a place! Can it be possible that scoundrel really met her? Surely Mary Faust would have guarded her as she did me! I must find the trail at once!"

Jim had been regarding him attentively. "Where did yer get de glad rags, boss?" he inquired. "Seems like yer was togged out in fire!"

Jack cast a glance over himself, and emitted a grunt of astonishment. His whole body except for his hands, and presumably his face was attired in little flickering flames, forming a complete suit or tunic and leggings, of becoming hues of green and brown. The flames, not more than half an inch in length, evidently proceeded from his flesh, though with no unpleasant effects—quite the contrary. Nor was this all. The herbage on which he stood was similarly on fire; the holes of the trees were alive with inner flames, and their leaves were individual tongues of colored fire. The very rocks that pushed up from the ground sparkled with an interior glow: and yet, in this universal conflagration, nothing was consumed, but only rendered brighter and more beautiful. Jim alone stood there unchanged, in what looked to be the identical suit of threadbare jacket and breeches he had worn in New York.

"Of course, Jim," said Jack after some thought, "we should expect things to be different on a different planet. We know that physical life is a sort of combustion, and here we can see it as well as know it—that's all. This is the way Saturnians dress, I suppose. But I wish we could see a few of them!"

"We'd best be humpin' oursel's, den," Jim suggested. "What's de course?"

"Suppose we try going west?"

This good young-American resolution was however delayed by the difficulty that there was no apparent way of determining which direction west was. The sun—where was the sun—too remote to be of avail; one could not say even whether it were day or night. Saturn, with its rings, lighted itself!

"Let's go straight ahead," decided Jack.

"Sure," assented Jim, and before they had gone a dozen paces, the gnome's sharp eyes had made a discovery. He pointed across the plain.

"A guy is headin' toward us, boss," he said. "Let's clear the decks fur action, till we fin's what he wants!"

CHAPTER IX
TORPEON'S MARK

THE newcomer was a pleasant-looking young fellow, of about Jack's age, and similarly attired, though in different colors. He came swiftly forward, with arm upraised in a friendly greeting. "Welcome, Jack!" exclaimed he. He laid his right hand on Jack's breast, over the heart—apparently the Saturnian mode of accost. "And this must be Jim," he added, smiling at the urchin: "you are welcome, both. Lamara, our highest, sent me to find and attend you. My name is Argon. I would have reached you sooner, but Torpeon, the arch mischief-maker, deflected your course hither, so that you landed far from the point where we were looking for you. Has he annoyed you?"

"We had a little argument," replied Jack modestly. "But he made an assertion as to a lady in whom I am interested, which gave me some anxiety."

"Miriam: yes!" answered the other. "She arrived here safely a few days ago, and Lamara assigned my sister Zarga to take care of her: Zarga is the best-loved and most trusted handmaid of the Highest. But Torpeon seems to have got information about her from some source yet undiscovered; there is even reason to suspect treason, and an investigation is being made. At any rate, he succeeded in gaining access to her at a moment when she was alone, and though he inflicted no actual injury, he was able to put his mark on her, which may suffice to put her to some inconvenience. Otherwise she is well, and eager, I needn't say, to meet her friend from New York."

"His mark!" repeated Jack, frowning. "What is that, and how does it affect her?"

"Torpeon is a skilful magician," said Argon. "Magic, among us, is condemned and forbidden as an evil; but we have learned to control nature by studying and adapting her laws. But magic is dominant on Tor: the Torides are an unruly and turbulent people, and for many generations they have been hostile to us. We never make war but we have means of passive resistance which are effective; so that though long ago the Torides used to make raids on us occasionally, they have now mostly given them up. Torpeon himself, however, sometimes comes here: and though he can do no hurt to us Saturnians, he is always on the watch for some visitor from another planet, who would be more subject to his arts. Miriam had come to us unexpectedly, and he laid a plot to kidnap her, with the idea, I presume, that she might be of use to him in his designs, which are very ambitious."

While Argon thus discoursed, he was leading his friends in the direction of a long, bright line upon the horizon, which might be the ocean.

"But the mark!" repeated Jack insistently.

"Torpeon carries with him a wand, which he uses for various

purposes," said Argon, "and he succeeded in touching Miriam once with it on the forehead. The effect it to put her, for an hour every day, into a sort of trance, during which he can communicate with her. The rest of the time she is herself, and her own mistress."

"And what is the hour?" demanded Jack.

"That is as Torpeon pleases: it may be any hour: we cannot control it, though our scientific men, under the guidance of Aunion, the chief, are studying means of dissolving the spell. But it seems very difficult.

Jack looked very gloomy. "I believe I know something of his wand," he remarked, indicating the truncheon which Jim still carried. "He fired a shot at me with it, but thanks to Mary Faust, it went astray. I wish I'd tried it on him."

"It would probably have been ineffective in any hands but his," said Argon taking the truncheon and examining it. "It is tuned to accord with the person using it. Your capture of it is a remarkable feat; but he no doubt has others. Mary Faust," he added, "is well known and greatly honored here. You are well protected."

"I'm not worrying about myself," returned Jack, "but Miriam."

"I feel sure that with reasonable precautions that will turn out all right," said the other. "Lamara will talk with you about it, and of course you will see Miriam. I hope you will like us and our world," he continued cordially.

"It's beautiful," said Jack trying to throw off his preoccupation. "I wonder it has so few inhabitants."

"Oh, there are plenty of us," answered Argon with a smile; "but we have no cities, as you do, and our habitations come and go as we need them: the permanence of your dwelling and structures seems to us strange and burdensome. My sister and I have made a special study of conditions on your earth. But as to our population, if you'll lift the visor of your cap, you will see some of them."

Jack had not been aware of a cap: but on turning back the visor he was startled to see that they were moving amid many groups of persons scattered over the landscape. They were cheerfully engaged in various occupations and amusements, and there was a number of pretty rustic houses, simple but commodious: but some of these, even while he looked at them, melted out of sight or disentangled themselves, as it were, from the special forms imposed on them by human design, and returned to the forest boughs, waving grass or other natural objects of which they had been composed.

"Is not this magic?" he exclaimed.

"No: only honest science. We have some control of the ether, and have solved a few other problems, so that our bodily needs are met with small labor. You will soon become used to us. Our discovery of invisibility was very welcome. It's only a matter, as you see, of reversing the direction of the flames, which are controlled by the cap. It put an end to the raids of the Torides: they find nothing but an empty desert."

"What sort of a place is Tor?" Jack asked, with a view to possible future adventures.

"Different from this: parts of it savage and dangerous, none of it beautiful. The greater part of the population is barbarous: the others, though highly trained in certain ways, live under a severe despotism. I have never been there myself; but it happens that my sister Zarga and I are descendants of one of the Torides, who remained behind here after one of their raids. That was many generations ago."

Jack's mind listened, but his heart, which was perhaps the greater part of him, was bent toward Miriam. He could find interest in nothing else. That one hour of each day under Torpeon's influence seemed to his lover's jealousy to lengthen itself into eternities. The passions of love and of hate raged within him.

Argon, perhaps divining his thoughts, said in a friendly manner, "Saturnians believe that the secret of happiness and power is power over one's self—self-command in all things. That leads to control over both matter and spirit. You, and Miriam also, are probably just now moved by strong feelings and wishes—personal impulses. So far as you yield to them, the influence of creatures like Torpeon finds access to you. Our wise men say that war against evil and wrong is always right, but that war against individuals who do wrong and evil is always a mistake: we must distinguish between the man and the evil in him. Then, he cannot harm us: otherwise, he may. It's a simple rule, but it needs discipline to observe it."

"It isn't so hard to bear trouble for one's self," said Jack, "but to bear it when some one you care for is concerned is another matter. If ever I get my hands on Torpeon again, I shall take a short way with him!"

"After all, he is more his own enemy than you are," replied Argon. "But I must confess I sympathize with your feeling. We will prevent him somehow. But—here we are!"

By some means not evident to Jack at that time, they had covered a great space of ground in a short while. They were now on a high, level space near the borders of the sea; a few miles from shore appeared a wooded island, with a tower showing above the trees: near at hand was an edifice of noble proportions, in front of which was assembled a small group of persons, foremost among them a tall young woman clothed in white.

"That is our Highest, Lamara," said Argon, in a reverential tone.

"But I don't see Miriam!" rejoined Jack, his face falling.

Argon made no reply, and they went forward.

CHAPTER X
THE TRANCE

LAMARA'S countenance was youthful, but luminous with intelligence, and her stately grace gave an impression of dignity and superiority. She was exceedingly lovely. She gave him the Saturnian greeting, together with a look of such amity and understanding as made him feel as if she had known him all his life.

"I wish your Uncle Sam and Terence Mayne had come with you," she unexpectedly said. "Mary Faust is always near us. Miriam is within." She turned to a lofty man of middle age beside her: "This is our chief councilor, Aunion: and this is my beloved Zarga, who lives close to my heart: I have chosen her to be with Miriam."

The girl thus designated was slight, and of striking beauty, with cobweb-fine hair of red gold hue, and dark eyes, which she had from the first fixed steadfastly on Jack. She was clothed in amethyst flames, like flickering violet petals. Jack, looking into those strange eyes, had a sensation of insecurity: mystery and fascination were in their unknown depths. But any misgivings as to Miriam's picked companion must be baseless. As her hand touched his breast, the light contact gave him the feeling that it had left an imprint there. She said, in a voice surprisingly deep, "I hope to make you happy!" and stepped back: but he was still aware that she observed him.

"You know too much of me not to know my errand here," he said to Lamara. "I hope your majesty will help me!"

"With all my heart!" said she, smiling. "We should be glad to have you and Miriam always with us: but your older friends need you. Argon will have told you of Miriam's mishap, which we hope is slight: we do not yet know how it happened."

She glanced at Zarga as she spoke. The girl addressed him.

"Miriam will tell you better than I: she had learned of your setting out hither, and when I was preparing the pavilion for her, she must have gone to the Planetary Mirror to get a glimpse of you. That exposed her, and Torpeon was on the watch."

"This mark—is it painful?" Jack demanded.

"It inflicts no physical pain," said Aunion, answering him in a kindly tone. "The chief effect, aside from the recurring periods of trance, lies in its rendering her less secure against further attacks. The results of a second act of indiscretion on her part might be serious. I found the mark resists ordinary means used to eradicate it: but if you and she are circumspect and patient, the spell will be overcome."

"We will go in," said Lamara, taking Jack's hand with a sympathizing look. "Zarga, go before, and find whether Miriam is ready to receive us."

Zarga slipped through the doorway and disappeared: the others followed. The room which they entered seemed large, but was so woven across with shafts of iridescent light as to disguise its dimensions: the semitransparent walls had the luster of mother-of-pearl. As they seated themselves on a divan, the light-shafts became denser until the party appeared to be enclosed in a pentagonal chamber of moderate size and great beauty. Lamara, observing Jack's bewilderment, laughed as might a child who had pleasantly surprised a friend.

"It's the same natural process that makes flowers grow," she said. "Add to earth and light something human from yourself, and deserts may become fertile and lovely. Such things as these, formed for the need of an hour, return of themselves to what they came from when the need passes. Our homes grow with us, never quite the same from one day to another. Science married to love works wonders."

She was interrupted by a cry from within, and in a moment Zarga appeared, her hair flying about her like a ruddy mist, and her eyes wide and ominous.

"The trance has come again!" was her announcement.

Jack sprang to his feet; but Lamara laid a reassuring hand on his arm.

"It is nothing," she said quietly. "Torpeon cannot pass the bounds of his license, though he may use it maliciously. He has chosen an hour close upon the last, but it will be the longer before he can disturb us again. Come, let us visit her."

She led the way to an interior apartment. In a room of oval shape, permeated with golden light, the form of a woman lay on a cushioned lounge, deep asleep. Her face was turned upward: her abundant black hair lay beneath her: the soft flames which draped her were of the hue of moss roses. In the center of her forehead was a small circular mark with a star in it center, red as blood. Her face was pale.

"Miriam!" Jack cried out, and was springing toward her: but Lamara restrained him.

"Do not touch her while she is in this state!" she said urgently. "For you to do so would be especially dangerous, because the results might be spiritual as well as physical. As you know, we have not yet solved the nature of the spell. This may be a trick of the magician to tempt you to involve her still deeper."

"But I love her! We love each other!" cried Jack; "Isn't love strong enough to overcome anything?"

"Love is unconquerable because it is an immortal spirit: but passion is mixed with earth, and seeks itself in the other. Power over evil is always from above."

The look and voice of Lamara, more than the veiled purport of her words, prevailed over the young lover. They carried conviction of truth. He mastered himself, and stood gazing with longing eyes at the motionless figure. He hated the material bonds that withheld him from communion with her soul.

"It is only for an hour!" said Lamara encouragingly. "When she wakens, we will all take counsel together. You overcame Torpeon; it will be more fruitful victory to overcome yourself."

"I must at least stay here beside her," Jack returned. "He might attempt something else: and it's my right to defend her."

"I will trust you," said Lamara, "because I perceive that there is more of spirit than of earth in your love: but there is earth, too, and remember that it is through earth that your enemy is strong! We will leave you here for a while: there are many things to be done to clear the way for your return to your world. Zarga will remain within call. Be faithful and patient!"

She withdrew, with Argon and Aunion. Zarga crouched beside the couch, her strange eyes dwelling upon the face of the unconscious figure. The beautiful features had the serenity and almost the pallor of death, but the slight rise and fall of the bosom was evidence that she lived.

Jack cautiously bent over to scrutinize the mark on her brow.

"It seems a slight thing to have so deep an effect!" he muttered.

"All magic is pretense," said Zarga looking up at him. "We may be deceived in the efficiency of this spell. Torpeon may count on that!"

"Can Lamara, you Highest, be deceived?" exclaimed Jack, surprised.

"You heard her say that the nature of the spell had not been solved. She is wise and prudent: but perhaps gives too much weight to Aunion's opinions. He, too, is wise, but age has made him timid. In their presence it didn't become me to speak."

"Do you know something they do not?"

"The blood of the Torides is in my veins," replied Zarga, "and it gives me an understanding of their nature which a pure Saturnian could not have. It led me, out of curiosity, to make a study of their magic, though secretly. We hold it to be unlawful, and instead of mastering its methods, we confine ourselves to seeking antidotes against it. I am foolish to have told you this—but I believe you are too noble to denounce me. My only wish is to serve you and Miriam, if I may. I think this mark could be easily annulled. Your own intuition about it was truer than our science." She met his troubled gaze for a moment, and added, "You said that love is enough!"

"Tell me all in your mind—you need have no fears!"

"Give me your hand," said Zarga. She took it between her own, pressing her left palm against his, and continuing to look into his eyes. He was conscious of a keen thrill or vibration that passed from her hand to his heart, and again from his eyes to hers, establishing a circuit between them. There was something sweet in it, but also perilous. He felt that there had been a disclosure, which might better have been avoided; and yet what could he apprehend from this girl? Lamara trusted her.

"You are what I thought," she said after a while, relinquishing his hand, with an enigmatic smile. "I will tell you my belief, and you can weigh its value in your own mind. Every moment that this mark remains on Miriam's forehead, its roots grow deeper, and the harder it will prove to take it off. Before Aunion's science can reach it, it will have become part of her being, which it would be death to disturb. Each swoon into which she sinks makes her more Torpeon's, and less yours. No one but the man who loves her can break the spell: and the time to break it is now! If the prince wins her from you, you can never win her back. Even her love for you will be destroyed!"

"That cannot be true!" answered he drawing back.

"Love is immortal: Lamara said it, and I know it!"

"I know nothing of immortality," Zarga replied, with a touch of scorn. "But whatever it be, I would not, if I were a man, wish to give the woman I loved to another during this life of earth!"

Jack's face flushed. "We can both die!" he said.

"Love wants life, not death!" the girl exclaimed. "Love has a body as well as a soul! Do you know that, while we sat here, Torpeon is with her? An hour of trance is his hour of possession! And how long will a woman love a man who stays inactive while she is in his rival's arms? Women love the possessor!"

He stood up, tense and trembling. The thought of his promise to Lamara fought with the passions that Zarga had aroused. But if Zarga's view were right, Lamara would withdraw her warning. What should he do?

Zarga seemed to read his mind. "It's not for a girl such as I to tell a lover what to do to save the woman he loves," she said. "But I warn you, if you touch her, Torpeon will exert his whole power to keep her. And don't think you can baffle him again as you did once! He will come with his legions behind him!"

Love, jealousy, and the pride of a man's valor against his foe, were temptations too strong: and at that moment Miriam stirred in her trance, her eyelids quivered and her lips moved. There came a muffled whisper.

"Jack—beloved—drive him away—save me—take me!"

She relapsed into immobility.

He was strung to the high pitch now. With love and wrath at once tingling through his nerves, he stooped to take Miriam in his arms: that mark—a kiss would obliterate it!

A shrill shout, which brought an incongruous image of Jim to mind, rang in his ears. A swirl of dark vapor filled the air. It seemed to him, however, that he held Miriam: he clasped her close. In the darkness, strange faces glared out at him and vanished. The woman responded to his embrace: she clung passionately to him. Yet there were both fire and ice in her contact, and Miriam seemed lost. Soft, fiery lips touched his, and fastened to them, they took his breath: he was buffeted, and staggered as if in a whirlwind. In the obscurity he had glimpses of other figures, and shafts of light, like swords, blindingly bright, struck through the dark. There were howlings and fierce outcries, receding and growing fainter, and a chilling gust dissipated the obscurity. The beautiful palace had disappeared: the scene was bleak and desolate; gravel and sand were underfoot and clumps of thorny bushes and stunted trees surrounded him. But he still held the form of the woman in his arms: they had failed to tear her from him; at least he so believed.

But she pressed her hands against his breast and writhed like a serpent to free herself. The cloud of hair that floated out from her in the wind was ruddy like fire. This slender, subtle face with its wild dark eyes—this was not Miriam! This was Zarga!

His arms relaxed and fell to his sides. She leaped away from him, and stood for a moment, throwing out her arms and screaming words which he could not distinguish: then she turned and fled away like a fantom, vanishing behind the thorny bushes.

He was alone in the wilderness. He took a step forward, and fell heavily on his face.

CHAPTER XI
THE ISLAND

"IS Miriam safe?" asked Lamara.

"She is safe for the present. But Zarga herself was the traitor," replied Aunion.

"The fault was mine! She seemed so lovable that I left her too much to her own unfolding. Why should she turn against us? And at such a time!"

"A spirit undisciplined—in whom impulses of nature, blameless in themselves, are prone under temptation to unite with the evil. Torpeon, as we now know, working on the kinship between them, long since began his appeals to her vanity and ambition; and the coming of these two strangers was his opportunity to strike. Miriam for him; Jack, in exchange, for her; and the stimulus of rivalry fired the inclination which she had already conceived for him. But for the warning given us by that singular little being, Jim, the plot would have succeeded; we arrived barely in season; and much mischief was wrought, not easily to be repaired."

"Where is Jack?"

"His transgression has isolated him; Argon is searching for him, with the more zeal because of his sister's treason. But we must face the facts: Torpeon's access to Miriam is easier than it was and more difficult for us to trace and prevent. Zarga, of course, is in hiding, and must be henceforth regarded as Torpeon's chief fellow conspirator."

"The strangers have at least one safeguard—they truly love each other!" said Lamara, after a silence.

"Else there were no hope! But the youth is prone to outbursts of lawless passion which the enemy will ever seek to provoke. We cannot constrain—only try to lead him. The conflict must proceed, with the odds on the Torides's side. Impotent though they are against us, against these two lovers, their arts and strategy are formidable."

"I believe Zarga can be redeemed!" said Lamara, meeting his eyes and speaking firmly.

Aunion sighed. "The constitution of our state is based on love and faith, and for many ages past there has been no provision for treason. Our strength is also our weakness. A thoughtless girl may sap the corner pillar and undo the growth of centuries."

"If the temple fall, it is that God may build a better!"

Aunion let his gaze wander over the scene around them. They were standing on the rocky promontory of an island near the mainland; the sea was calm and mirrored the great arch of the ring. Groups of heavy-foliaged trees shadowed the soft turf; the music of their leaves mingled with birdsongs; staglike animals moved here and there in the glades, and more rarely other shapes, swift and graceful and semihuman, peeped shyly forth from shade to light. Beyond, above the trees, rose the dome of a summer pavilion. Over all the island passed breathings of wild-flower perfume like fairy music.

"God indeed has enabled us to incarnate the substance of our minds," Aunion said musingly; "to shape them after our thought and to color them with our emotions. Others painfully toil against the obduracy of things to accomplish what we may do and undo with the flowing of a breath. Their works, rude parodies of even the crude conceptions that inspired them, crumble slowly back into unsightly dust. They have never called upon what is above to interpret what is below; they exalt the slave into the despot, and fight one another for monopoly of what closes life against them and opens death. And yet these blind ones survive, while our Eden may be blighted by the guile of a serpent and a girl's folly!"

"But these blind ones fight toward the light!" rejoined she, with a touch of reproof in her tone. "Their serpent is ours too, and they, grappling with it in blood and tears, bear our burdens as well as their own. God's meanings are manifested according to the measure of the eye that sees; but He never misleads! He will not punish the misstep of a child by the banishment of a people!"

"I have perhaps lived too long," said Aunion sadly. "The inspirations of your heart are more trustworthy than the speculations of my brain. What do you now intend?"

"I shall stay by Miriam and incline her toward the deeper consciousness where Torpeon cannot penetrate. Argon will inform me here of his fortune in the search of Jack."

"I will hold myself in readiness to aid either of you," said Aunion; and with a reverent obeisance he parted from her.

Lamara took a path to the pavilion. The island, and all on it, was the place of private retreat for the young sovereign of Saturn, and was guarded by influences framed to repel all unauthorized intruders; only the initiates could enter. Thither, accordingly, Miriam had been conveyed from the scene of the conflict between Jack and the powers swayed by Torpeon. The prompt putting forth of exceptional resources had been required to accomplish this without injury to her; for had her trance been broken before the lapse of its period grave harm might have resulted. The situation, as it now stood, was perplexing; but Lamara felt confident that time and prudence would bring a happy solution. The conspirators had failed of their main object; and it was not to be supposed that Zarga would venture to cooperate in any further designs. Jack, though wofully misled, was still strong in his unalterable fidelity, and he would find redemption at last.

It was the revelation of Zarga's perfidy that wounded Lamara most. Some rare quality in this girl's soul had induced Lamara to give her her fullest confidence; her faults had seemed trivial and superficial. A certain adventurous independence of thought sometimes perceptible in her had given Lamara no uneasiness; it was due, she fancied, to the abounding in her of life too vivid to submit unquestioningly to the guidance of an elder experience. There was in the somewhat tumultuous nature of her youth the making of a great and noble character; and Lamara had often forborne reproof in the belief that Zarga's own afterthought would administer a severer chiding. Yet now she stood convicted of an unpardonable crime.

No human soul, however, could sin beyond the limits of Lamara's forgiveness. She might have harbored hopes even for Torpeon. And she would not divest herself of the belief that her favorite Zarga would yet repent and make amends.

At the spot on which the pavilion stood a spring gushed out of the ground, the abundant waters of which had been curiously led to run into architectural surfaces and forms—a plastic crystal forever flowing away with a pleasant murmur. The changing lights of day united with it to create continually shifting hues, and the gentle coolness which always reigned in its chambers aided to make it Lamara's favorite place for rest and meditation.

Here, as being beyond all likelihood of disturbance, she had caused Miriam to be conveyed; no invader from Tor would dare to set foot on any part of the island, still less to violate the sanctities of the pavilion itself. The hour during which the trance prevailed was now for some time passed; but she had wished her visitor to awake alone in the translucent solitude, and to recollect herself under its soothing influence. She had planned that her own approach should take place at a moment when the girl should begin to feel anxiety as to what had befallen her.

Passing the threshold of the edifice she entered a small atrium, opening at the other side into an enclosed court. In the center of this played a fountain, whose upgush assumed successively various forms, treelike, animal or human. Several chambers surrounded the court, and in the central one of these Miriam had been laid.

Stepping lightly and smiling with pleasant anticipation, Lamara advanced to the door of this chamber and looked within. It was empty!

She repressed her first impulse of surprise and uneasiness, telling herself that Miriam must be somewhere in the pavilion; or might, at most, have wandered out along the winding paths that threaded the surrounding coppices and glades. She prosecuted her search with ever-increasing misgiving. The pavilion was untenanted. She came out into the garden, passing hastily through its lovely intricacies, but found no trace of the fugitive. The birds flitted after her with their songs, the fawns gamboled about her, and the shy little nature-people smiled and beckoned to her from nooks and leafy recesses. All things loved Lamara, and she loved all; but the beautiful earth-girl was nowhere to be seen.

Only initiates of the mysteries could either enter or leave the island unaccompanied. Only Aunion and herself had been there that day with Miriam. Yet Miriam had vanished.

What could have happened?

CHAPTER XII
THE SECRET EXIT

MIRIAM'S trance was physical only; and the disjunction of spirit from body was not so complete as to prevent occasional gleams of consciousness from passing from one to the other. But normal cooperation was suspended. The spirit, however, was beyond Torpeon's reach, and his power over the body was limited to reducing its functions to quiescence. A far greater effort would be required to bring the living and conscious woman herself under his control. Such an effort, in the Saturnian environment, must prove futile; and all his art and ingenuity were therefore bent upon the enterprise of transferring her to his own place.

The plan of his attempt at the palace had been well and boldly laid, and Zarga had played her part efficiently. But in failing to consider an element in the problem so apparently humble as Jim they had committed a radical error. His devotion to Jack and Miriam was single-hearted and unreserved, and it had sharpened his insight into possible sources of danger. Zarga had aroused his suspicions from the first; and the fact that she was trusted so implicitly by the others served to render his own watchfulness only the more keen.

He had observed, while Lamara and her party were preparing for departure, leaving Jack and Zarga alone with Miriam, that one of the attendants, at Lamara's direction, had transmitted a signal to the island through a certain instrument attached to a pillar of the portico of the palace. His fondness for mechanical devices had caused him to examine this contrivance after they were gone, and though the principle on which it worked was unlike anything he had seen on his own earth, he perceived readily enough by what means it was operated. He now applied himself, without compunction, to observing as well as he could what was going on between Jack and Zarga in Miriam's chamber; and what he saw and heard augmented his suspicions of the girl's good faith. He had almost made up his mind to send a signal to the island, on the chance that it might bring assistance, when, happening to glance upward, he saw the red planet Tor directly in the zenith, and, detaching itself therefrom, an object bearing some resemblance to a parachute, which sped toward Saturn with the swiftness of a meteorite. He delayed no longer, but with all his force pushed in the rod or plunger which had seen the attendant use. At the same time he gave vent to the scream, which Jack had overheard. The next instant he was bowled head over heels by what seemed to be a blast of fiery air; and he did not recover his senses until after the ensuing conflict was over.

We follow the movements of Zarga. Terrified and enraged at the miscarriage of the attempt, and at the ruin involved to her personal hopes, she had fled away, not heeding whither she went, until she was arrested by the towering figure of Torpeon in her path.

"Back to Tor, Prince!" she cried, "and take me with you. All is lost here!"

"No; now is our best chance for success!" he returned, with fierce resolution. "The moment to strike home is when the enemy believes you defeated. The youth shall be my care; do you follow the woman. She has been take to the island, where they believe her secure; none can enter there but the initiates; but you are of the inner circle, and your privilege has not yet been canceled. Hear my instructions and follow them, and every end we aimed at will be gained. Throw aside all scruples; your career on Saturn is closed forever; you have nothing more to lose here. But I will make you great on Tor, and the man you love shall be at your feet. You are of my blood; be worthy of your lineage!"

"I fear nothing, because I hope nothing," replied the girl gloomily; "but I am willing to make one trial more. He will never love me; but to part him from the woman he loves will be some consolation. Tell me your plan."

"With beauty such as yours, and opportunity, no man can resist you," said Torpeon; "you will need no help from me; but in serving you I shall serve myself. Listen to me and I will show you how fortune fights for those who defy her!"

After conferring together they separated, and Zarga made her way toward the seashore. Torpeon, after some minutes of intense thought, betook himself in another direction.

Miriam, in the soft silence and seclusion of the pavilion, drew a long breath and opened her eyes. Her first thought was of Jack, whom she had been preparing to meet at the time the trance overtook her. But this room, with its silvery gleams, was different from the one which she last remembered. She turned her mind back over the sequence of events since her arrival on Saturn. She recalled Zarga's having told her of the planetary mirror, in which distant events were reflected; it might show her her lover, who was even then on his way to seek her. Unaware of the conditions under which alone the mirror could be safely consulted, she had unhesitatingly entered a small domed structure sunk in the solid rock which Zarga had designated. There, in the darkness, she had first discerned nothing; but presently she had seen, set in a metal frame, an oval object having the appearance of a giant eye, mysteriously luminous, the inner circle of the pupil black, and enlarging its diameter as she gazed into it. In those depths there were indistinct movements, evolutions, glimpse of things approaching and withdrawing, wide wastes of space; and the shining out of stars; the waving of trees in the wind; the foam of falling waters. Suddenly the circle of the pupil was filled with a ruddy glare, and seemed to grow immense; she was looking on the surface of a planet, wild chasms and pinnacles, the spouting of volcanoes, the rush of boiling waters. The figure of a man with shaggy black hair and fierce eyes appeared in the midst of it, sweeping toward her with incomprehensible velocity, a scarlet mantle waving out from his herculean shoulders. Now, apparently his actual self stood before her, his gaze meeting hers; in his right hand he carried a short staff that glowed like molten metal. He pointed it at her forehead; she felt a sensation like the touch of flame; she had seemed to sink down, and knew no more.

After an interval, of what duration she knew not, she had revived to see faces bending over her—Lamara, Aunion, Zarga, Argon; Zarga wringing her hands distressfully and speaking volubly; the others compassionate and sympathetic. What had happened?—some inadvertent transgression, some catastrophe; Torpeon's Mark! She had put her fingers to her forehead and felt the circle there. "It is not irreparable—it will pass away!" she heard Lamara say, in her gentle, reassuring tones.

After that a kaleidoscope of minor occurrences, ending with news of Jack's arrival, and his expected appearance at the palace. She was awaiting the moment of meeting; Zarga had entered. "He is here; come!" She had joyfully started up and had taken a step forward, when all at once blankness had closed around her, and her next consciousness had been of this wakening in the island pavilion. What had intervened? And Jack—where was he? She sat up and looked about her.

From her present position she could see the fountain in the court, the singular movements of which concentrated her attention.

The clear waters were molding themselves into the likeness of two human figures, which appeared as if locked in a desperate struggle. They might have been carved by a master-hand out of pure crystal, except for the constant and lifelike contortions and writhings that they exhibited. At first she had no thought of recognizing in these effigies any resemblance to persons she had seen before; but as the struggle continued a suggestion—a persuasion—possessed her mind that she knew them—they represented Jack and that shaggy giant who had confronted her out of the planetary mirror! They were engaged in a life-and-death battle; and it seemed that the giant was gaining the advantage.

No sooner had this impression become fixed than the two figures dissolved into the natural flow of the fountain, which, for a time, appeared no otherwise than an ordinary water-jet. But ere long it began to assume another form, this time of a woman—a young girl, of lightsome and graceful form who, with arms outthrown and floating hair, seemed to be dancing joyously toward her. Surely this apparition too was familiar! It could be no other than her friend Zarga!

What caused these moldings and transformations, Miriam, of course, could not conjecture, though she knew something of Saturnian powers; but the second presentation relieved her somewhat of the forebodings stirred by the first. She had never been made aware of any reason for distrusting Zarga—quite the reverse; and it seemed probable that if these watery creations bore any relation to real persons and event, Zarga's lighthearted mood portended some beneficent sequel to the menace of the first scene.

But, on the other hand, perhaps her imagination had altogether beguiled her! And now the fountain relapsed once more into formlessness.

A snatch of song echoed through the court, and Miriam turned to see Zarga herself come tripping airily into view.

"Come, come, come!" she sang; "all is ready, and I am sent to fetch you! The boat is prepared; Jack is waiting for you to get aboard; the others are assembled to bid you farewell. So fair a day might not come again in a lifetime! But we must make haste! Come, come!"

Miriam had involuntarily risen, and Zarga, taking her by the hand, was drawing her toward the door of the pavilion. "We must make haste!" she repeated.

"But how did this happen?" she asked. "Does Lamara know?"

"Lamara! Does she not know everything?" exclaimed the girl, laughing. "And isn't this a wonderful adventure! I wish you could have stayed with us longer—or I wish I might go back with you to your earth! Would any man there love me and marry me, do you think? Are there any men there like your Jack?"

"Many men might wish to marry you," replied Miriam; "but there can never be but one Jack! Is he well and happy?"

"He will be happy when he sees you; just now he is very impatient!" answered the other. They had left the pavilion and traversed a deeply-shadowed path, while these remarks were passing, and were now descending a slope which led to a flight of steps cut out of the rock. These terminated in a cavern.

"Why, we are underground!" exclaimed Miriam, drawing back. "Where are you taking me? Can this be the right way?"

"It is the shortest," said Zarga, urging her forward. "They are awaiting us at the other end."

The cavern was a natural excavation in the rock, winding to right and left, now narrow and low, now high, expanding into great chambers columned with stalactite and stalagmite, and sometimes resounding with noise of subterranean waters. The rocks emitted a dim light, sufficient to dispel the darkness and enable them to go forward rapidly. But Miriam could not help a sensation of disquiet; this was a strange beginning of a journey through space! She observed a feverish excitement in Zarga's bearing. She was about to remonstrate when the path, which had hitherto either descended or proceeded on a level, took an upward inclination, and a draft of warmer air set steadily against them.

"We're near the end," said Zarga; and hollowing her hand before her mouth she sent forth a long call. It was caught and reduplicated by innumerable echoes, floating away, to be again and again renewed, as if prolonged by a myriad vocalists. When it had finally died away there came an answering note, deeper and stronger, falling upon the ear in rising and subsiding cadences. Zarga glanced back over her shoulder.

"Your lover answers us!" she said.

The answer had not seemed to Miriam to have the quality of Jack's voice; but the echoes might have disguised it. The passage widened out, and the unmistakable light of day flowed in. But as Miriam lifted her eyes the first object that met them was the red globe of Tor suspended up yonder in the sky.

"Are you sure there is no danger?" she asked, halting.

"Come, come!" cried Zarga, dragging her upward almost with violence. "We are late already! There's not a moment to lose! Come!"

But a conviction that something was amiss suddenly came over Miriam.

"I will go no further!" she said.

But her determination came too late. They were now within a few paces of the entrance; and there appeared before her the figure, not of Jack, or of any of her other friends, but of him whom she could not fail to recognize as Torpeon. He smiled as their eyes encountered, and extended toward her the truncheon in his hand. She felt the mark on her forehead burn, and power to resist forsook her. She was drawn forward in spite of herself.

The aspect of the prince was stately and stern, intellect mingled with passion in his imperious countenance. His expression softened as she drew near, and conveyed a desire, the intensity of which made her tremble.

But indignation at the ruse played upon her kindled her to defiance.

"You may make my body obey you," she said; "but not my soul!"

"I know the limits of my power," he replied. "I had no means but this. If I fail to prove my right to you, I am too much a king to take what is not given. Come to my kingdom, learn to know me, and decide."

"I can never love you; do not make me hate you," said Miriam.

His heavy brows quivered for a moment.

"Love or hate—we will prove which is stronger; come!"

Disdaining futile resistance she stepped into the car that awaited them; he took his place beside her, and they rose in air, headed for the red planet. Zarga, left below, gazed at them till they were out of sight; then, with a mocking wave of her hand toward the island she went inland.

CHAPTER XIII
FALSE TRAILS

JACK'S subjection to the power of mortification and despair did not last long. He raised himself from the ground and stared about him. The first thing he saw was Jim squatting before him.

"We was sure up ag'in a tight squeeze dat time, boss," remarked his retainer. "Did yer hear de yell I let loose? Dat big guy in the red sweater was a comin' head-on! But our folks had heard de alarm, an' before I gits knocked out I seen 'em hot-footin' up de trail. I guess dere was some scrap; but which side gits de decision is more'n I knows. But say, boss, I ain't got much use fer dat yaller-haired kid. Looks ter me like she double-crossed yer. Ain't dat right?"

"Jim," said Jack, getting on his feet "what we must find out is, what became of Miriam. Did you see anything of her?"

"Not me, boss; I was takin' de count."

"We're worse off than we were before," remarked Jack. 'I suppose I behaved like a fool; but things are puzzling here. If Argon, or somebody, would help us out!"

"Mebbe dat's him now!" said Jim, pointing across the desert.

Jack wheeled round and looked. Something was approaching and at a good pace. It had the look of a vehicle of some sort. Jim, after eying it intently, shook his head.

"Dere ain't a traffic-cop on Fif' Av'noo would stan' fer dat outfit!" he declared.

As it drew near its make-up was revealed. The vehicle somewhat resembled the two-wheeled chariot of classic times: the driver stood in front; but instead of a pair of horses the shafts were attached to a metal sphere about four feet in diameter, which rolled and bounded onward, in obedience to a motive-power apparently contained in the sphere itself. The vehicle drew up beside them, and the driver, an odd-looking creature, with a big head, staring eyes, and a copper-colored skin covered with course hair, motioned to them to get aboard.

"Say pal, where did yer blow in from?" Jim inquired.

The driver shook his head and pointed to his mouth, which he opened widely. There was no tongue in it.

"The fellow is dumb!" ejaculated Jack.

"It don't look right ter me," observed Jim. "Let's side-step it!"

"He is evidently sent to fetch us somewhere," returned Jack. "We can't be more lost than we are; and who but Lamara can have sent it? We may as well get in—there's nothing else in sight."

"It's up ter you, boss," said Jim doubtingly, "but it sure is a phony rig! I'd like ter know what dat there ball has inside it!"

Jack had already climbed into the vehicle. He reached out a hand for Jim, but the driver had set the contrivance going, and it was only by an active leap that the little cripple succeeded in making the connection.

They were off at full speed.

"Talk about speed-laws!" said Jim, after a moment; "dere ain't no limit on dis geezer! What you got dere, pal—a balloon?"

"Something of that kind, I should say," observed Jack quietly. In fact, the car drawn by the metal sphere was actually rising from the ground. They were soon several hundred feet aloft, and still on an up-grade.

"No doubt it's all right," Jack added; "he's getting his bearings like a carrier pigeon; he'll make a slant for home presently."

The driver, however, was not following a straight course, but was bearing continually to the left. It soon became evident that they were mounting on a spiral. The planet was fast dropping away beneath them.

"What is the dumb beast doing?" muttered Jack in surprise. "Does he think he lives in the air? He must come to earth sooner or later."

Jim had been taking observations on his own account. He now plucked Jack by the arm and reached up to whisper in his ear:

"Boss, dis slob ain't comin' down at all. D'yer know where he's takin' us? He ain't no Sattum guy whatever. He's one of Torpy's gang, and he's elopin' wid us to where Torpy come from!"

At this startling suggestion Jack looked upward and beheld the red moon which was Torpeon's habitation directly above them. He had been fooled again; it was a plain case of kidnaping! Had he been aware that Miriam was at the same moment being unwillingly borne in the same direction he would probably have been content to let the flight proceed; as it was, he thought it was time to take an active part in the transaction.

He seized the driver by the shoulder with a powerful grasp.

"Put about!" he shouted. "Get back to earth! Reverse your machine this instant or I'll throw you out!"

The driver, however, was strong as a gorilla. He squirmed out of the grip of Jack's hand with comparative ease and gave a twist to the rod which connected with the sphere and served him as reins, with the effect of making the mysterious motor ascend more swiftly than ever. They were now at least a mile about the surface.

"Dis ain't no healthy place for wrastlin', boss," Jim suggested. "Better lay low a while and catch him when he ain't watchin' out."

But Jack's blood was thoroughly up, and he was in no mood for procrastination. The question in dispute should be settled then and there.

"Hold on tight, boy," he said to Jim; "I'm going to teach this gentleman better manners. He may be a better man than either Torpeon or I, but he'll have to prove it."

Without further preface he sprang upon the copper-colored driver, and a furious fight began. The creature struggled like a wild beast. All limitations of civilized, and even of human warfare, were abandoned; if his tongue were missing, his teeth were like those of a cave bear; and both hands and feet were armed with nails that looked like the talons of a griffin, and were used as such. He shrieked, bit and tore, leaped up and down, threw himself into unimaginable positions, got his shoulder under Jack's thigh, and fought frantically to throw him on his back. Failing this, he got him round the body with his gorilla arms and, disregarding the tremendous blows which Jack dealt him, strove to fasten his fangs into his throat. The car, meanwhile, swayed from side to side like a skiff in a hurricane, and threatened to overturn every moment. Just then a swinging blow, driven with all the power of Jack's arm which might have felled an ox, caught him fair on the jaw and broke it; and at the same time a vigorous thrust from Jim's crutch, which he had been watching his chance to deliver, struck him in the left eye, and doubtless put it out of service.

With a hideous screech the monster relinquished his hold of his adversary and flung himself out of the car. It looked like suicide; but that was not the design of the gorilla from Tor. He came face down upon the metal sphere, and gripping it fast between his knees, disconnected with his left hand the guiding-rod from the car. The sphere, with the creature on it, continued its ascent with added impetus, and was soon far away; while the car containing Jack and Jim began a descent toward the planet beneath.

The situation seemed serious. "I think we're in for a bad tumble, Jim," Jack remarked, glancing over the edge of the car. "It's some comfort to have landed on that fellow's jaw before he got away; and that punch you gave him in the eye will help him remember us; but Saturn will hit us a harder blow yet. If you should happen to come out alive tell Miriam we did our best."

"Dat tumble we had from N'York was bigger dan dis, and didn't hurt us none," Jim responded cheerfully. "Some o' dem Sattum guys may be holdin' a blanket to catch us, like at a fire on the Bowery. Say, boss," he added, "here's dat keepsake de lady give yer in de lab'ratory hangin' down yer back! What about it?"

Jack had forgotten the sapphire talisman. If it had warded off the lightning bolt launched at him by Torpeon it might have some further occult virtue in reserve. The drop earthward continued with increasing velocity, but there was still a good distance to go. He lost no time in getting his hands on the talisman, and there it lay, sparkling in his broad palm. But how was it to be used?

"Look at what's comin' for us, boss!" squeaked Jim.

Some disturbance had occurred in the atmosphere—a vortex movement, reminding Jack of a Kansas tornado he had seen in his boyhood. It swooped down upon the car with a long, whistling scream. The vertical line of their descent was immediately modified, and they were driven off in a circular direction, like a boat gyrating on the circumference of a whirlpool. The little talisman blazed like a purple star. The car still approached the earth, but was so buoyed up on the wings of the tornado as greatly to counteract the attraction of gravitation, and the angle of incidence was so much enlarged that they would strike the surface at but a slight deviation from the parallel. Even this, however, might give them an awkward jolt, for their speed was immense.

"Hurray, boss, we're saved!" called out Jim, with a gesture of triumph. "We gits a bat' an' dat lets us out. Pipe de lake!"

In fact, they were skimming toward a handsome sheet of water, with tall trees grouped along its margins; at its further side rose a lofty butte with perpendicular walls that gleamed like crystal. In another moment the car struck the lake near its center, and was carried along by its impetus, amidst showers of spray, at a pace which no electric launch could have rivaled. Before the impetus had exhausted itself they had been brought within a few rods of the shore; as the car came to rest Jack stepped out midleg deep in the water, took Jim on his shoulder, and waded to dry land. The tornado had vanished overhead.

"Coney Island can't beat it!" Jim observed as Jack set him down.

"It won't bear talking of," said Jack gravely. He had passed through emotions during the last few minutes, the effect of which he would never lose.

They looked about them. The crystal butte was close at hand, and almost in its shadow stood a small cottage with white walls and wide-spreading eaves. A vine bearing heavy clusters of yellow flowers climbed over its porch; the door stood invitingly open; the casements were spread wide; and on the clear air was spread a fragrance which caused Jim to assume the attitude of a hound scenting quarry. His face was lifted, his nostrils sniffed eagerly, and his little black eyes, half closed, gave to his countenance an expression of dreamy voluptuousness.

Jack, whose olfactories had been slower to awake than his companion's, looked at the urchin in astonishment. "What ails you, boy?" he demanded.

"Oh, gee, lead me to it!" breathed Jim in an unctuous murmur. "Delmonnikers never smelt like dat! Eats, boss, eats! Gimme two dozen hot dogs an' ten plunks wort' o' ham-and, an' keep de change! Lead me to it!"

By this time Jack had caught the odor, and he emitted a long-drawn "Ah-h-h!"

The perfume, rich and delicate, swam on the air and seduced the senses. With it came the realization that not since leaving New York—it might be days or years ago—had food passed his lips. No wonder if his heart had sunk under the blows of fate! Not Hercules his labors, Archimedes his inventions, or Terence Mayne his New Madison Square Building, could have been accomplished on an empty stomach. His appetite, as the odor continued to insinuate itself, dilated to heroic proportions. A kingdom for an ox roasted whole!

"Foller me, boss!" chanted Jim in gluttonous tones: "I's on de trail!"

He was hobbling incontinently toward the cottage, which bore a touching likeness to the annex-bungalows of terrestrial summer hotels. From its chimney climbed gently upward a column of bluish smoke, which was dissipated about by languid air currents, winged with deliciousness. Jim reached the door first.

But with sublime self-restraint he halted there, poised on his crutch till his master should enter. Jack caught him up under one arm, and the next instant they found themselves staring at a table exquisitely arrayed in white damask, porcelain dishes, sparkling flagons, and glistening silver. Gracing these utensils was royal abundance of delectable soups, juicy meats, fragrant vegetables, quivering jellies, mounded cakes and fruits, the bubbling promise of vintage wines, and on a side table an urn of incomparable coffee. Lucullus was outdone!

The two adventurers seated themselves opposite each other, and Jack proceeded to do the honors. "Clear turtle, Jim," quoth he, ladling out the golden liquid; Jim had already begun to fill his mouth with *hors-d'oeuvres.* "Our appetites need no stimulus, but a sip of this amontillado will spiritualize them. Turbot, I declare! I wish Uncle Sam were with us! No, let us limit ourselves to one help—that pheasant must have full justice! Perhaps the venison outdoes the sirloin, magnificent though that looks; and the burgundy harmonizes with the noble stag. A little of this jelly! Do you smoke, Jim? While we are breathing ourselves for the pudding, we might try one of these cigarettes. Jim, you are looking better!"

"Dis is heaven, ain't it boss?" Jim inquired.

"A part of it, I hope. A glass of this champagne will fortify us for what is yet to come. Sip it reverently—it is the apotheosis of the Widow! I incline to the pie rather than to the pudding—unless you are adequate to both. I am but a man—you, a boy! I envy you! After all, even a banquet so transcendent as this serves but as preparation for the coffee and cigars. What are you saying?"

"De yaller-haired kid, boss!" Jim whispered. "She's pipin' us t'rough de door!"

Jack turned and beheld the smiling face of Zarga.

CHAPTER XIV
THE MAGICIAN'S HALL

ZARGA did not wait for the banqueters to recover from their surprise, but came forward at once with the air of a hostess conscious of having pleased her guests. Her bearing seemed so artless that Jack, rendered genial by the good fare, told himself that there must be something amiss in his recollection of their last meeting.

"I tried to make a dinner for you that would remind you of home," she said. "We Saturnians don't use food of this kind. Are you satisfied?"

Jack had risen, and could think on the spur of the moment of no better answer than the polite banality, "Only your presence at the table could have improved it!" while Jim seized the opportunity to stuff a couple of red apples and some sugar-coated cakes into his pockets.

"We ought to have waited to learn who our benefactress was," Jack went on, being somewhat embarrassed; "but I thought only how hungry I was, and how providential—"

"Providence lets us help it sometimes!" she interrupted, laughing. "One must feel lonely in a strange country; but in their hearts all people are alike."

Here Jim ventured an observation.

"I guess, miss, my boss t'ought you an' Miss Mir'am was some alike dat time de blizzard hit us, back dere!"

Jack turned red; but the girl merely looked amused.

"I supposed it was one of your terrestrial customs," she observed. "Oh, it doesn't matter a bit; your kisses were delightful!"

This was putting the shoe on the other foot. Jack could not get the red out of his face, but he was glad to absolve this friendly little creature from the charge of unseemly boldness. After all, was it not he who had made the mistake?

"How did you know where we were?" he asked, to get the conversation on less ticklish ground.

"Oh, we know, when we want to," she replied. "I remember Argon's telling me you have only five senses where you live. We have some others besides, which we can use or not, as we like; just as we can either walk to a place, or be there right off. I prefer to be there right off, as a rule," she added.

"So would I, if I knew how!" rejoined Jack with emphasis.

"There are two ways—the proper way and the magic way," she said. "The magic way is not proper; it's fun, though, sometimes!"

"I should think any way proper that got me to Miriam," Jack affirmed. "I was searching for her when I found the dinner!"

"But you were glad of the dinner!"

"You said it, miss!" put in Jim. "But now we've got it stowed, we're hot on de trail agin!"

Zarga glanced from one to the other, and seemed to hesitate.

"You haven't heard, then?" she asked at length, in a tone of serious concern.

"Nothing. Have you any news?"

Zarga, with an impulsive gesture, put out her hand and laid it on his. "Do you love her very much?" she asked.

"What has happened?" exclaimed he, pale enough now.

"And she promised to love you always?" Zarga went on, looking him deep in the eyes.

"What is all this?" he demanded, a menace beginning to growl through his tones.

"Don't be angry with me!" she entreated tremulously. "I wouldn't hurt you for the world! I'm sorry—I will say nothing more!"

"I ask your pardon," he said, controlling himself. "Please tell me all you know. I had heard that Torpeon was pursuing her; she is to be my wife; you can imagine my anxiety! The only glimpse I've had of her was when you—"

"I understand! I thought perhaps Argon or Lamara would have told you. But why did they not tell you? Why should they leave it to me?"

"I haven't seen them since they left the palace to go to the island. Then—you know how it was; there was a sudden storm of fire and darkness, and when I could see again, everything had disappeared, and—you were in my arms!"

"Yes, yes! Oh, I was frightened! The fire got into my brain. Yes, I ran away, forgetting you wouldn't know where to go. But Miriam was rescued by Aunion and taken to Lamara's island."

"She is safe, then?" cried Jack joyfully.

"Now I shall have to hurt you," she replied sadly. "She is there no longer. Torpeon sent her a message; she met him, and they went off together to Tor."

"Who told you this silly lie?" he demanded wrathfully.

"I was there myself. I did all I could. I couldn't prevent her."

Jack was silent; she glanced timidly at him, then hid her face in her hands and began to sob. But Jim, who had been staring fixedly at Zarga, now touched Jack on the elbow.

"Don't yer worry, boss," he whispered. "De kid is stuffin' yer. She's nutty on yer herself—dat's what!"

Jack, in the tumult of his emotions, neither heard nor paid attention; the counsels of wisdom are often rejected because their source is humble. Zarga moved slowly toward the door.

"Don't go!" said Jack huskily. "Torpeon is a clever conjurer; he deceived you as well as Miriam, I suppose. To Tor, you say?"

"Do you trust me?" she faltered.

"I'm sorry if I was rude. In thinking of my enemy I forgot my friend. I never needed friends more than now."

"It would be my happiness to make you happy," she said, coming closer to him. "But it's best to know the truth. I can show them to you, if you wish!"

"Show them to me—in Tor?"

"I must break our law to do it; but our laws don't bind you, and I don't care for myself! I know the magic of the Torides; and if you are willing, and have courage, I can make them appear before you as they are at this moment. It's for you to say!"

"You can show me Miriam and Torpeon here and now?"

She took him by the hand, led him to the door of the cottage, and pointed to the great butte.

"In that rock there is a secret chamber, made by a great magician, in the times before the Saturnians abandoned magic. It has been sealed since his day, but I know the way to enter it. There is danger, but for me only, not for you! If you fear nothing, and do nothing violent, I think no harm will happen."

"I don't fear the truth; and there's nothing else to fear," said he.

They went forward toward the foot of the huge cliff, which towered thousands of feet straight upward; its smooth and massive front seemed beyond mortal power no less to penetrate than to scale. Within arm's reach of it Zarga paused.

"Only you and I may enter," she said to Jack; "a third would be fatal to us all."

"Jim can wait in the cottage," said Jack, turning to the little cripple. "You've had your dinner, Jim, and we'll return before you're hungry again."

"Me stummick ain't what's troublin' me, boss," Jim replied; his misgivings had by this time become acute. "I kin pass up de eats, ef de lady'd gimme a ticket fer de gall'ry."

But his master shook his head with a kindly look, and the urchin, greatly dejected, was fain to obey. He turned and hobbled back toward the cottage.

Zarga laid her slender hand on the rock. No crevice had been apparent; but as she pressed lightly against the surface, the crystal walls yawned slowly apart, making an opening large enough to admit them. She motioned Jack to enter; he stepped within unhesitatingly, and she followed. The opening closed behind them, but Jack, who had already gone on, found himself in a corridor, vaulted high, winding into the interior. Underfoot was a smooth floor of sparkling, white sand. Light pervaded the place, clear and mild, like that of the moon. Zarga was now beside him. He felt her soft fingers close on his own.

"Do not let go my hand till we reach the chamber," she whispered. "The guardians left by the old magician are here, and would try to mislead you or to bar the way. None but I has been here since he departed. But they know me, and I have the clue."

"Your hand is like fire," murmured Jack; "what makes it so?"

"There is fire in my heart; when we are together, it burns," was her reply. "Now be silent; we are nearly there."

While Jack was speculating as to the significance of her answer, the walls swept apart, and he found himself in a circular hall about a hundred feet in diameter, the domed roof of which was lost in the moonlight dimness. Its perfect symmetry showed it to be human handiwork, though he could not conceive by what means the adamantine hardness of the crystal had been hollowed out, and the walls carved with devices so strange and so exquisitely wrought. The light here had a faint bluish tinge, which enhanced the solemn impressiveness of the monumental figures ranged at regular intervals round the chamber, supporting the entablature of the dome. Their faces were veiled and their heads bowed; in the molding of their bodies the human flowed into the animal; but whether man were descending into beast, or beast rising into man, could not be determined. At times it seemed as if the flux were even now proceeding, with the issue questionable. Between the figures were arched panels carved in intricate designs, perhaps symbolical and mystic; here the hues of the crystal varied prismatically through ruby, emerald, sapphire, chrysoprase and topaz. The room was paved with yellow and purple slabs disposed in coiled patterns that suggested the slow writhing of serpents; in the center stood a pentagonal block of black stone, with a circular depression in its upper surface, like a baptismal font. But it was filled not with water, but with ashes.

There was a crescent-shaped bench in front of the font, with a high back, and arms fashioned like the heads of serpents. The seat was deep, and fitted with cushions; the material was massive silver. Over one end of the bench was flung a scarf of fine tissue, gray, like smoke, and almost as diaphanous. After Jack, complying with Zarga's indication, had seated himself, she caught up the scarf and with a movement of her hand caused it to revolve about the slender grace of her figure, as if emanating from the violet flames that clothed her body. Her hair spread itself out on the air as she began the steps of a slow dance, voluptuous and wild as that of the antique Bacchanals. Had Jack's mind been less painfully preoccupied, he must have admitted that no vision so alluringly beautiful had ever floated before his eyes.

After thrice making the circuit of the font, Zarga stopped, and the scarf, continuing its movement, wrapped itself lightly about her. She stooped, and seemed to gather up from the pavement at the base of the font a double handful of flakes or chips, which she placed in the hollow of the stone. They at once kindled and smoldered, sending out an aromatic scent. A column of thin blue vapor rose straight upward, till it impinged upon the apex of the dome; and a deep but soft strain of music vibrated through the hall.

The incantation had begun to work.

CHAPTER XV
A FRIEND FROM THE STARS

AFTER Jack and Zarga had disappeared into the butte, Jim wheeled and hobbled back to the place where he had parted from them. It had been his intention, in spite of orders to the contrary, to slip in after them, and take a hand in whatever might be going to take place. His boss, though the first of mankind in Jim's estimation, was not qualified to take proper care of himself.

But he was confronted by the impenetrable face of the rock, with not a crack in it large enough to admit the point of his crutch. Miracles did not perplex Jim, but they sometimes annoyed him. After eying the rock disgustedly for a few moments, he hit the great cliff a reproving tap, and retired to a small boulder hard by and sat down upon it. If the persons in whom he was interested came out by the same way that they had gone in, he would be on hand to receive them. Meanwhile, as his dessert had been interrupted by Zarga's arrival, he took one of the apples from his pocket and began to munch it appreciatively and philosophically. "Dat kid ain't straight, but she puts up a good feed," was his judgement.

Before the apple had been half consumed, a plashing noise from the direction of the lake caused him to look around. Had he been Achilles or Alexander the Great, instead of a one-legged New York newsboy, the sight that met his eyes might have alarmed him. As it was, he was merely filled with a wary but delighted curiosity.

Jim had once upon a time visited the Museum of Natural History in New York, and had there, in a large saloon, beheld a plaster model of an amphibious animal which had lived, wallowed, and devoured eight million years ago. It was seventy-five feet long, twenty-five feet at the shoulder, and displayed the scaly terrors of a tail which was only less fearsome than its neck and head. Jim wished at that time that he had been born soon enough to have pursued the original of this model with a repeating-rifle and a snickersnee.

Here, now, was the animated and active grandfather of the comparatively trivial and pygmy reptile which had been revealed to him in New York. It was so big that it might have entered the category of geologic phenomena, and held its own against a range of hills. The girth of its forelegs was as that of a giant sycamore in a Southern swamp; the row of ridges down its back might have served as a fence against a Hun invasion; its jaws yawned as wide as the portals of the church of Saint John the Divine in New York; each one of its double row of several hundred teeth was as tall as a drum-major and as sharp as the blade of a Louisiana colonel's bowie; its tail was for the most part veiled by the lake, but the end of it was stirring up whirlpools as far out in the water as a second basemen could fling a ball. The whole creature was advancing upon Jim with the gladness of a familiar friend; and though its gait was leisurely, it was able to cover an acre of ground at a stride.

It did not occur to the boy at first that the apparition was meant especially for him; any more than he would have regarded the annual procession of the New York police-force up Fifth Avenue as having been organized with an eye to his capture. The disproportion was too preposterous. Of what consequence could he be to it? A mosquito might as reasonably have looked upon itself as an adequate meal for a crocodile. But it did not take him long to modify this view. There was no viand other than himself in sight, and he had seen a lizard engulf an ant with apparent pleasure. He must stand upon his defense!

The most feasible plan that occurred to him on the spur of the moment—a spur, in this case, of exceptional urgency—was to take a sprint along the animal's tongue and reach the comparative safety of its gullet before it could bring its teeth to bear upon him. But he was handicapped by his one-leggedness; nor, should he win to the interior, had he so much as a pen-knife to chop his way out again. Running away would be equally vain; and to side-step the charge of a creature with such a tail was to invite disaster. The two or three seconds which he devoted to these reflections had sufficed to bring his antagonist so near that the next waddle would be the final one, so far as Jim was concerned.

Jim stood up, supporting himself against the boulder, and holding his crutch at arm's-length vertically before him. The crutch was a stout bit of blackthorn, and sharp at one end. If he could contrive to thrust the crutch between the animal's jaws at the moment they closed upon him, it might happen to pierce the roof of its mouth, and the prick thus administered might give him a chance to slip out before being crushed to a pulp. The stratagem did not promise very well, but it was the best he could do.

"It's a good job the boss ain't here!" was Jim's last thought. He looked down a glutinous abyss which seemed to extend to the bottomless pit itself. "Come on, old sockdolager!" he shouted.

A slender shaft, arrowlike, and bright as lightening, flashed before his sight and struck the stupendous snake-lizard fair in the eyeball. There it stood, buried to half its depth, quivering. With such a missile did Olympian Jove quell the revolt of the Titans.

The effect was not to be compassed by mortal senses. Jim was blown backward by the foul expulsion of the creature's breath, executing involuntary catherine-wheels over a space of a dozen yards. He picked himself up to witness a convulsion in which earthquake, tornado, and waterspout seemed to outdo their utmost. It was accompanied by a scream which made the roar of a volcano seem to Jim's ears like the whistle of a boy's pipe. As the creature flounced and flung its hideous length, the waters of the lake fled away, the solid earth groaned and was riven into crevasses, and a boulder as big as a bungalow, caught in the coil of its tail, was flung upward till it looked no larger than a pebble, and when it fell again it was splintered into gravel.

What followed was, if possible, more surprising. The contortions ceased as suddenly as they had begun, and the animal lay flaccid and inert, a flood of blackness, like liquid pitch, oozing out between its jaws. As this went on, the bulk of the enormity shrunk rapidly, and the poisonous darkness of its coloring faded to a pallid, brownish hue, like a crushed tarantula. It shriveled, diminished, and disintegrated; and in a few moments all that remained of it was a heap of brittle fragments dwindling into formlessness. The lake flowed back over its bed and resumed its limpid serenity; the trees stretched their boughs over the turf, and the birds twittered and sang their tranquil music. It was difficult to believe that the late terrific uproar had been more than an evil dream.

Jim recovered his crutch, and then became aware of a personage standing a few rods away on the right, leaning upon a spear, and thoughtfully contemplating the scene of the late cataclysm. He was stately, strong, and clean-limbed, and in the prime of his youth. There was such a brightness in his aspect that it seemed to Jim that he cast a radiance around him. He recognized him at once as Solarion, who had shown his prowess in the battle with the Jovians. He hobbled toward him with an appreciative grin.

"You is sure Johnnie-on-de-Spot, mister, an' you fetches de goods!" he exclaimed earnestly. "Dat big critter t'ought he had us locoed; an' along you comes, quietlike, and pastes him one in de eye, an' where is he?"

"You did the hardest part of the work yourself, Jim," replied the other, smiling. "A stout heart is the best help in any battle. But I happened to have a dart in my hand, and I couldn't resist letting it fly. What are you doing here—and where is Jack?"

Jim gave a terse account of their recent adventures. "So de boss is jugged wid de skirt inside dat mountain," he concluded; "an' me, I's waitin' till dey comes out to take a han' in de game. I ain't got no use for de yaller-haired kid; all de same, dis strangle-hold she's got on de boss is mebbe a good t'ing. He ain't got no prudence; an' her keepin' him in dere keeps him out o' trouble, wedder or not she means it. He's al'ays set for a scrap, my boss is; ef he'd been here, he'd 'a' gone fer dat beast, sure, and got hurted. Now he's huntin' Torpy, ter git Miss Mir'am away from him; but what I wants is dis—an' mebbe you kin give me a lift! While he's safe in de mountain, you puts me over on de red moon, ef dat's where she is; an' I figgers I'd come near getting' her free. But ef I slips up, an' Torpy gits me—all right! De boss comes right along an' makes his spiel; an' at a straight show-down he kin knock Torpy over de ropes. But Torpy, he has funny stunts ter burn, an' he might git a fake decision ef de boss ain't put wise fust. An' den, I arsks yer, where 'd Miss Mir'am git off?"

"Your idea is, then," said Solarion, "to take the risk of getting killed first, in order that Jack, profiting by your experience, may have a better chance of rescuing Miriam? But why should you run your head into danger that brings you no reward, even if you win?"

Jim bent upon his interlocutor a serious and reproving glance.

"Say mister, youse ain't playin' up ter yer form! Lis'n here! My boss is some man, ain't he? I guess yes! An' he's mushy on Miss Mir'am, an' she on him; an' dey's goin' ter do de orange-blossom an' rice act fust t'ing dey hits N'York. On de udder han', what am I good fer? Do I know anyt'ing? Am I a collidge guy, an' play full-back on de team? Is dere any skirt campin' on my trail? G'wan! I'm tellin' yer dis worl' is goin' ahead right smart widout me! So what I says is, keep de boss here till me an' Torpy has it out togedder; an' while he's busy lammin' me fer keeps, snake Miss Mir'am out o' dere and han' her over to de boss. Dat's all! Dat's me! Dat's right, ain't it? Are yer on?"

Thus Jim spoke, with snapping eyes and graphic gestures; and as Solarion listened he became brighter and brighter, until Jim's small person cast a long shadow behind him.

"Your plan is good," he said, "and I'd rather be in your shoes than in Torpeon's. We get what we are willing to pay for. May I have a look at that crutch of yours?"

"She ain't so nifty to look at," Jim remarked, handing it over; "but she does me all right. My dad, he brings her from de ould sod!"

Solarion examined the crutch with great attention.

"I don't think you know what a valuable stick this is," he said at length, returning it to the owner. "There are fairies in Ireland, you know; and when they gave this blackthorn to your father, they endowed it with a power to do wonderful things. It's a fairy wand, and it will make itself into anything you want—a sword, a horse, a pair of wings, or an air-ship, for instance. All you have to do is rub one or another of these little knobs, and make your wish. If you want to go to Tor, it can carry you there easily; and then, if you find it necessary to fight Torpeon, I dare say you could surprise him as much as I surprised that beast just now. That's what comes, you see, of having only one leg!"

Jim looked at his old familiar staff with new respect. It appeared the same as ever; but great gifts often go humbly clad.

"Say, mister, dat's goin' some! Yer ain't stringin' me, is yer?"

"We receive only what belongs to us," returned Solarion, laying a hand on the boy's head. "You are among friends, and you've earned their friendship. Good-by for the present, and good fortune!"

The light grew brighter than ever; but when Jim looked up, he was alone.

CHAPTER XVI
THE LASSO

LAMARA, having convinced herself that Miriam was no longer on the island bethought herself of the subterranean passage. This was a secret way to the mainland, and known to few; but one of those few was Zarga. There was no escape, therefore, from the conclusion that the girl had taken this means of continuing her treachery; but Lamara hastened to explore the cavern, and found abundant traces of the passing of both Zarga and Miriam. On the shore at the other side there were signs that sufficiently indicated the rendezvous with Torpeon and the flight to Tor.

Lamara's intuitions, which were of the highest order, had given her a knowledge of Miriam's heart and character, which obviated any doubt that Miriam must have been hoodwinked. But the problem of how to rescue her from her unwilling thraldom remained. The traditional usages of Saturn discountenanced aggressive action; but neither had any situation similar to this been anticipated. Unprecedented needs require the exercise of corresponding methods. Had the problem been simply the subjugation of Torpeon, and of his kingdom with him, there were resources in Saturn adequate to accomplish it; but to do so without involving Miriam in danger would be far more difficult. Torpeon would hesitate at nothing, and if driven to extremity would not scruple, Lamara feared, to sacrifice Miriam rather than surrender her. Nor was this all. Lamara had reason to suspect that he contemplated an enterprise which, were it successful, would carry him and his abode beyond the limits of Saturnian influence. It was an enterprise wild and desperate, and it might result in the annihilation of Tor itself, not to speak of serious disorders in other planets of the system. Lamara divined that his determination to keep Miriam might urge him on to the immediate prosecution of this gigantic and reckless scheme; and it behooved her to lose no time in taking measures to prevent it. Aunion and others must be consulted; meanwhile she resorted to the planetary mirror, which was in the neighborhood, to ascertain the actual present condition of affairs.

Upon entering the sunken dome, she pronounced the formula proper for her purpose, and subdued her mind to observe what should transpire.

For a few moments the eye was dark and vacant of images; then the blurred traces of a rapidly moving object appeared; it was focused an instant later, and Lamara saw Torpeon and Miriam on their way through space. The prince glanced behind him at intervals, as if from a feeling of insecurity. Miriam, her black hair flying behind her like a banner of mourning, sat motionless. What could be the cause of Torpeon's uneasiness?

The fugitives were still within the outer confines of the Saturnian atmosphere, and approaching the ring. The vast, shining curve of the latter was in such a position that they were silhouetted against it, and every detail of their aspect and surroundings was distinct. The ring radiated sublimity; it was composed, as Lamara knew, of the crystallized bodies of those who had passed to another life from Saturn; an immeasurable mausoleum and memorial of the friends who had departed. Billions of mortal forms, in which souls had once lived and loved, were here spontaneously disposed in their innumerable ranks, enlightening the world which they encircled in ever-augmenting myriads. Each atom of that solemn army sparkled forever in its appointed place, and contributed in its degree to the far-flung splendor. And in some eon too remote for calculation the mighty circle would disintegrate to form a new and radiant planet, on which would be born and flourish and fulfil its destiny another and nobler race, to carry forward to another stage the majestic evolution of humanity.

Lamara sighed. For this divinely appointed scroll of death and life, made to remind mortal existence of the immortal future that awaited it, was now serving as the background to reveal the lawless act of a self-seeking and finite ambition. The trail of carnal passions defiles the pure pavements of the holy temple!

Her meditation was interrupted by an unexpected episode.

Into the field of vision was suddenly projected a long loop of azure light, tenuous as a spider's web, uncoiling itself like a lasso, aimed to overtake and encircle the flying pair. Lamara immediately recognized it as a thread of power thrown out by some Saturnian pursuer to arrest the progress of the robber prince and his captive.

"It is Argon!" she murmured the next moment, as the figure of the youth swept into sight. "It is a gallant effort; but I fear he is too late. Even did it succeed, the peril would be great!"

Unless the feat could be accomplished before Torpeon could pass beyond the Saturnian atmosphere, it would be useless to attempt it. The chase was now nearing that boundary; and the risk to Miriam of a contest in mid air was obvious.

The first cast of the aerial lasso failed, passing ineffectively to one side. Argon, who had unfolded the wings which every Saturnian may employ at need, gathered up his shining line and prepared for another trial.

But Torpeon had already become aware of his predicament. The car leaped forward with redoubled impetus, causing it to sway dizzily from side to side. Miriam, aroused from her apathy by the singing of the noose, had now turned and realized what was going on. Her friends were trying to save her. Far down in the void she had seen the pursuer; the distance seemed enormous, but it was lessening. She took a breath or two to make up her mind.

Meanwhile, she controlled every expression of emotion. Torpeon, indeed, had no suspicion of her intention. He was employing all his energies to pass the pale of danger. From the corner of her eye Miriam saw the pursuer swing his arm for another cast. Should this fail, she would act!

Lamara, intently observing, discerned not the outward manifestations merely, but the thoughts which produced them. She knew Argon's activity, courage, and address; but the hazard was too great. Yet to intervene now was impossible.

Keen like the note of a harp-string in the shrillest treble came again the sound of the noose. It reached its highest pitch, and the noose itself appeared above their heads, opening and descending. Every nerve in Miriam's body was drawn tense for the outcome. Down came the shining circlet, carrying its message of defeat for Torpeon or of liberation for her. So truly had Argon estimated the distance that it seemed certain they would be taken. But Torpeon's skill and foresight were not less than his.

Just as the shining cord settled around them, Torpeon, by a titanic effort, brought the car to a halt. It dropped straight downward, leaving the slip-knot to close empty above them. By another wrench at the guiding shaft he caused the vehicle to swerve violently to the left; then to start forward once more. The snare had been evaded!

The moment for Miriam's attempt had come. She had been thrown on her knees by the sudden turning of the car; she steadied herself, and then sprang to her feet. The car staggered in its course; for an instant the sky seemed to reel; the ring flashed before her eyes, dipped, and vanished; the vast globe of Saturn impended above her head, and she caught a lightning glimpse of Argon halting in his flight, and watching, appalled, for the issue. She summoned all her energy, and leaped from the car.

What might be the consequence, she had not cared to consider; there was the chance that Argon might intercept her fall; there was the possibility that she might join the silent army of the ring. It was even conceivable that, at this immense distance from the planet, she might be borne away in an orbit of her own, and journey forever in an endless spiral through the fields of space. Anything would be preferable to enduring the dominion of the prince of Tor.

But Torpeon, though he had perhaps not anticipated a voluntary act on her part, was not unprepared for the event, and was ready to meet it. With a resolve as desperate as Miriam's, he flung himself headlong after her as she leaped.

For the duration of a single pulse-beat, the twain hung in mid air, the gravitational force of Saturn, diminished by the counterpull of Tor, operating but feebly. Ere it could gather strength, he had thrown an arm around her. She felt its grasp, and struggled fiercely against it, but in vain. The car, dropping with them, was within reach of Torpeon's other hand. He caught it, and still holding her, dragged himself aboard. Once more he sent it flying on its way. The bounds of Saturnian influence were passed, and Argon's pursuit had failed.

Torpeon turned his head, his face so close to Miriam's that his beard brushed her cheek, and searched her eyes with a look that pierced like a sword. In that glance was manifested the whole savage strength of the man. The car sped on, and presently became a mere speck in the mirror. The figure of Argon, descending, flashed into view, and Lamara left the dome and went forth to meet him.

CHAPTER XVII
THE WINGED HORSE

ARGON, on alighting, was encountered by Aunion, and the two were soon joined by Lamara. Argon bowed before her with a mortified look.

"I blundered from beginning to end," he remarked.

"You did your best," she replied; "none can do more, but the spirit rules the outcome. No just cause is lost through our effort to win it; it is gained, though in ways beyond our comprehension. The good we try to do may bless us even more through failure than success. It may be that to have brought these two lovers together before the appointed time would have delayed instead of hastening their final union."

"I hoped to compensate for the mischief done by my sister," he said dejectedly.

"That child has beguiled us all," said Aunion. "I could almost wish that these visitors of ours had never come here. Strange influences create strange conditions, which disturb our ancient peace."

"You are out of tune!" exclaimed Lamara. "If a new era awaits us, let us accept it with faith and joy. The birth of all good is preceded by travail. The destiny of the Saturnians cannot be separated from that of any others in the universe. If there be evil anywhere, isolation cannot heal it; it must be nursed back to health in the bosom of love. I do not regret our visitors; I welcome them, bring what they may!"

"Zarga has sinned beyond forgiveness," declared Aunion sternly.

"I have already said that I find myself much to blame for her error," returned Lamara quietly; "and judgement does not lie with us, old friend. Already her sin brings its own punishment. Jack's constancy is inviolable; but we may remove him from her influence for both their sakes. Were you able to trace him?" she asked Argon.

"Torpeon and Zarga, working together, had made discovery difficult," he said; "but I was close upon them when Miriam's danger drew me aside. I believe I know where to find Jack and my sister. But the magician's chamber is well guarded."

"It is time those spells were broken," said Aunion.

"Is the little lad, Jim, with them?" Lamara asked.

"I think not; I fear he has met with misfortune."

"That child is very near my heart," Lamara said. "Every thought and impulse in him is free from self. We must protect him with all our power. His love and loyalty are without stain; they shine through his quaintness like flame through a grotesque lantern."

"Jim will play his part," Aunion affirmed, with a smile. "It is my impression that he has found a powerful friend—Solarion himself!"

Argon had a hand to his ear. "Isn't that the piping of the Nature people?" he exclaimed. "Yes—yonder they come! And Jim in the midst of them!"

"You are right—they are leading him in triumph!" rejoined Lamara gladly. "They feel the innocence and honesty of his soul; it is a high honor to win their affection. His goodness has found him out! But what can be his errand?"

"We shall soon learn; the imp has the gift of tongue," observed Aunion amusedly.

The festive group drew nearer. Jim's stature was not great; but he loomed large by contrast with his retinue. The little creatures came skipping and gamboling around him, all in high spirits, and evidently much pleased with their companion. Fauns and nymphs, hand in hand, danced and cut capers; satyrs were piping heartily on their reeds, interrupting themselves now and then to turn head-over-heels; the company had gathered flowers as they came, with which they made wreaths to decorate their new friend and themselves. Jim managed his crutch so deftly that the lack of a leg seemed to be no handicap; he hopped and pirouetted almost as nimbly as the others, and his jollity was as wholehearted as theirs. He greeted Lamara and her friends from afar, grinning wide.

"Hello, folks! What d'yer t'ink o' dis bunch? But wait till I learns dem pipers ter play 'Yankee Doodle'!"

"You find them good company?" asked Lamara smilingly.

Jim did a comprehensive gesture.

"Dis here hull joint is like de pantomimes down in de Bowery; when yer t'inks yer's up ag'in trouble, de ceilin' busts t'rough an' down swoops de fairy wid de goods; or de stage splits up, an' dey yanks down de vill'in out o' sight. An' de elf kids hops out of de bushes an' give yer de glad hand. Yes, sir, yer has de game down fine! It's sure some class, Sattum is; but lil, ol' N'York has yer beat, at dat!"

While Jim thus expressed himself, his retinue withdrew a little, and watched the tall human creatures with shy curiosity.

Lamara stooped and gave the urchin a kiss. "And where are you going now?" she asked.

Jim reddened and glistened under the tribute; but recovered himself.

"Me? I's out fer blood!" he announced. "I leaves de boss ter tackle de yaller-haired kid, whilst I starts fer Torpy. I figgers you folks kin look out fer dis end of de line; but Torpy, 'tends ter him meself!"

"But how will you get to Tor" Argon asked.

"Don' let dat worry yer, young feller! I ain't much ter look at; but I meets up wid dat shiny gink—Sol Something he calls hisself—yer knows who I mean—he comes along, frien'ly like, an' swots de big lizzud I was arguin' wid; an' after we've chinned fer a spell, he gives me crutch de once-over, see, an' allows dere's a hull kit o' tools in her, what de fairies put dere; but I has a guess dat he done it hisself! Anyhow, she's loaded fer bear, an' when me an' Torpy gits inter de ring, dere'll be somp'n doin', believe me!"

"Is this possible?" Argon asked Aunion in an undertone.

"I cannot interpret," he replied, shaking his head.

"We may trust Solarion—he is of a higher order," said Lamara. "Still, something disquiets me on the child's account. But it is not for us to hold him back."

"Well, folks, I's on de war-pat'," Jim said, handling his crutch in a peculiar manner, "an' now I's goin' ter giver yer a s'prise! Kin'ly turn yer backs, all han's, till I makes me prep-rations; an' don' look eroun' till I gives de word! No peepin' now! Abbry-cadabbry! Presto change! As yer was! What d'yer t'ink o' dat?"

The others had indulged his humor, and now faced about again. How it had happened only Jim and perhaps the little Nature people could have told; but there Jim sat on a superb black stallion, which tossed its head, shook out its tail, and unfolded a pair of wings so wide and powerful that they seemed capable of bearing him from one end of the solar system to the other. The beautiful creature danced impatiently on its dainty hoofs, and seemed eager to be off.

"Well done, Jim! Good fortune! Safe return!" they cried; and the Nature people set up a joyful shout.

Jim settled himself in the saddle, and handled the reins with professional assurance. "Keep yer eye on de boss!" were his last words. He waved his hand, the horse gave a mighty sweep with his wings, and steed and rider bounded splendidly into the air.

CHAPTER XVIII
THE BLACK MAGIC

JACK, seated in a corner of the silver bench, kept his eyes upon the column of blue vapor that rose upward from the smoldering fire in the font. But his mind was filled with somber thoughts of Miriam, and he was only superficially conscious either of the incantation or of Zarga. Of Miriam's faith he had no doubts; but as little could he question that Torpeon had by some means contrived to convey her to his stronghold. He could not think that Zarga would willfully mislead him upon that point, though he had indignantly rejected her suggestion that Miriam had consented to it; the idea that the Saturnian maiden was herself infatuated with him could not find entrance into his straightforward mind; his own simple loyalty kept him from suspecting others. What the incantation might reveal was a matter of conjecture, but he did not so much as allow himself to imagine that it would present Miriam in any other light than as the soul of love and faith.

The music swept out in penetrating waves, the notes vibrating insistently upon the ear with a sweet but almost intolerable monotony; but the monotony gradually became a source of fascination. It seemed to enter into his blood and control the pulsations of his heart; it had the effect of a seductive but suffocating perfume, against the influence of which one might struggle at first, but at last found an exotic delight in yielding. It soothed the outward senses, but wrought a strange excitement within. Zarga had resumed her mystic dance, and now he followed her movements with dreamy intentness; she had ceased to be a distinct personality to him, but was a part of the general scene, and represented in movement what the rest imparted by color, form and sound. Her body and limbs, exquisite in their supple eloquence, swayed and shifted like the waving of slender fronds in tropic gardens, or the rhythm of fairy surf lapsing on coral beaches. She seemed far away, yet thrillingly near; and her face, as it was recurrently turned toward him in the turnings of the dance, had the spell of beauty alternately revealed and withdrawn into the magic shadows of memory. He felt the gaze of her dark eyes more poignantly in its absence than when turned upon him.

Once more the dancer halted suddenly, with arms uplifted, and the music sang its insistent song no more. There came a volley of staccato sounds, as of a startled nightingale, and the column of vapor was agitated and broken into revolving wreaths. These twisted themselves together, forming huge figures vaguely outlined, lit by fitful gleams from the embers in the font. Zarga turned and ran swiftly toward Jack, crouching, and pressing her fingers against her temples. "It is coming—it is coming!" she cried; "put your strength round me—let me come inside your arm! I am afraid of what I've done!"

Jack, disconcerted, drew himself erect on the bench; but the vaporous forms now shaping themselves above the font so commanded his attention that he hardly noticed how Zarga nestled against him, warm, panting, and tremulous, like a bird seeking refuge; how her head lay on his breast, and the flexible fingers of her hand touched his face and wound themselves in his hair. His arm was about her, and from an involuntary protecting impulse he patted her shoulder; but he was absorbed in the scene before him.

The smoke-figures, condensing, appeared no longer gigantic, but assumed the stature of life. Two human apparitions were together, a man and a woman. More than their sex could not at first be determined; they sat facing each other in a deep alcove, disclosed by a semblance of draperies that hung on either side. The coloring of life, faint in the beginning, gained depth, as if an artist were adding to his gray outline more vivid touches from his palette. The living picture acquired each moment greater definition; from point to point the outlines and contours settled into certainty; and Jack's lips grew dry as he recognized more and more unmistakably the proportions and movements of the woman he loved. For the other figure he had as yet no eyes, but he knew it could represent no other than Torpeon. His beloved, and his enemy, seated there face to face and hands in hands!

"It is false!" a voice spoke thus in the remote recesses of his soul; "a false profanation of what is sacred!" But the terrible persuasiveness of the vision overwhelmed him. The testimony of the sight, fallacious though it so constantly be, dominates the nobler assurances of the spirit; and the very struggle against the illusion causes it to take on outlines more convincing. Miriam's face was latest to be revealed. The look it wore was the look of love in its passion; and it was lavished not on him, but on another!

Torpeon had taken both her hands in his, and was speaking with imperious urgency. Unconsciously, Jack strained Zarga's hand in his, and his heart beat tumultuously against hers. Miriam's eyelids fell as Torpeon pressed his appeal; her deep bosom rose and subsided in irregular breathings; by an effort, she partly turned herself away; but it was the last struggle of resistance, and her lover would not be denied. Slowly she faced him again and lifted her eyes to him; Jack ground his teeth as he saw that look. Her body relaxed and was inclined toward the pleader, with the loveliness of yielding in her smile. With a proud gesture his arms went around her, and he drew her to him; his bearded mouth met her parted lips. Jack sank back in his seat with a groan. Clouds drifted in before the picture, and it faded out and was gone. The vapors melted away, and the black font's embers dulled into grayness. Zarga, her arms round Jack, had drawn herself up, so that her smooth cheek rested on his, and her breath touched his lips.

"Noblest and dearest," she whispered, "I would have saved you from this grief and shame; but her wickedness must be seen to be believed. It is better to know than to doubt; she is not worth your grieving; she was never worthy of you; she would have betrayed you, whether for Torpeon, or another. But if you will see what love is, forget her, and look at me!"

Jack's brain slowly awoke to the meaning of these words, as if he returned from a long and dreary journey. "What has happened to the world!" he muttered.

He raised himself deliberately, like a man who regains consciousness after a swoon. He took her wrists in his hands, and detached her arms from their embrace. He held her off and looked at her, sadly and searchingly.

"It is all illusion," he said; "this and the other!"

"There is no illusion in my love!" answered the girl, in a deep murmur. "I loved you from the first moment. Had her love held true, I would had died and kept silence. But she betrayed you and I have shown you the secret that is myself! Yes, look at me! Am I not beautiful? What happiness is there that I cannot give you? Take me—know me—love me! In this world there are a thousand joys that are not dreamed of on your earth! And our years are not few, like yours, nor can age dull and enfeeble us. My power is great; I will lead you through endless delights, blooming one after another, like roses from one stem of love. Or if you long for daring deeds, mighty works, or strange adventures, fame and worship, I can launch you on such a career as no tales of heroes tell! You are made for the highest things; do not let yourself sink down before the treason of one woman! Let us live and love together, and we need not wait for death to show us immortality, for our every moment shall be immortal!"

"I know nothing of all this," he said, in heavy tones. "What you think of me is all amiss. I'm a very ordinary creature. I love Miriam, and she loves me—that is the whole of my world and my life. We can have only one sorrow—to be separated from each other; and we want no other happiness than to be together. These visions that we have been seeing—they oppressed me for a moment; but they are gone, and they are nothing. Love is once and for all; after that, there can be no changing or choosing. It has taken what I am and given it to Miriam, and what she is, is in me. I could as soon become another man, as love another woman; I can see that you are beautiful, Zarga; but beauty is nothing to me, except as Miriam's beauty is a part of Miriam; and I love it as a part of her. And what are endless delights? For her and me there is only one delight—our love—and that is endless; we want no other. Works, adventures, fame? My love makes me a man; and no other adventure or achievement compares with that. Miriam's safety and happiness are my work and adventure; and for that I am here. Don't imagine such an insanity as that you can love me, or I, you! If you will be my friend, set me on my way to save Miriam from the trouble that has befallen her; neither you nor I are foolish enough to be deceived by a smoke-wreath, no matter what images some magic-lantern may throw on it!"

Zarga faced him with clenched hands and burning eyes.

"I tell you once more, she does not love you; she does not even love Torpeon; she yields to him only because he has made her believe that he can make her queen of all the planets. Her heart is as cold as a burned-out cinder; will you, with your heart of molten gold, waste yourself on her?"

A frown began to gather on Jack's brow.

"You must not say these things," he told her, sternly. "They are not true, and I don't think you yourself believe them. I've been here too long; I will stay no longer. If you will help me to find Miriam, I will be very grateful; if not, let us part now!"

"No; you and I will never part," she replied, in a changed voice. "I have offered you myself, and I will never let you go forth to boast of it, or to find another woman. I have brought you to the center of this rock; none but I knows how to enter it, and none can pass out from it but by my leave. Here you shall stay until you die; and I will stay with you. You say I cannot love you; I love you, and hate you, enough for that! When the end of the world comes, and the graves are rent asunder, they will find our bones here, intertwined like lovers. Let Miriam make what she can of that!"

"You have not the power to do what you say," answered Jack. She stood between him and the entrance to the hall; he put her aside with his arms, and went forward.

But before he had advanced three paces, darkness sudden and absolute descended upon the cavern. It was like no other darkness; it was as if he had been all at once closed about by some black substance that molded itself to him like the matrix to which it holds. All sense of direction was lost; it even seemed as if he knew no longer which was below and which was above. There were whisperings in his ears; soft, mocking laughter, the padding of naked feet, long soughings of drafts through unseen crevices. He attempted to go on in the way he had started; but a few steps, carefully taken and measured, brought him up against the solid wall of the crystal rock. He set out to circumvent the chamber, remembering its circular form, and keeping one hand in touch with the wall; but after journeying for a thousand paces, more than enough to account for more than ten times the circumference of the chamber, he had arrived at nothing; there had been no interruption in the adamantine smoothness; for aught he could tell, indeed, he might have passed into some passage leading yet deeper into the heart of the butte. Again he tried to cross from one side to the other, in the hope of finding the black font, from which he might take a fresh departure; but after many minutes, with every precaution not to deviate from a straight line, he had come to no end; he might have been traveling across an empty and lightless desert. The sounds which he had at first heard had now died away, and an appalling silence had descended, like another darkness; and yet, dogging his footsteps, close behind him, invisible and inaudible, but felt something following him relentlessly; something hostile and formless. What was it? Starvation? Madness? Death? Once he wheeled suddenly and leaped with outstretched arms to grasp it. Nothing!

At length he ceased his futile efforts and stood still, with folded arms. He gathered up the forces of his will, and quieted the throbbing of his heart, which had become vehement and irregular. There was no escape; he would face that fact and accept it. Famine and death; but there should not be madness! The light of the body was gone; but the light of the mind should endure. No fear, or longing, or despair should banish from his thoughts the image of Miriam and his faith in their love. He had bought these at a great price, and he would never give them up. This was the end of his great adventure; he would meet it with the constancy of a true man.

Hark! A sound like the rising of a mighty wind; a rending and shuddering as of the throes of earthquake! The cavern rocked; the foundations of the mountain were shaken. A flicker of light divided the blackness, and at the same moment soft arms were thrown round him, and a bosom, palpitating with terror, pressed against his own. Zarga's bosom, and her arms!

Before he could free himself, she uttered a wild cry and staggered back, pressing her hands over her heart. She stared at him in amazement and dismay; was that blood upon her fingers? The sapphire talisman still hung round Jack's neck, and it sparkled vividly, sending forth rays like keen arrows.

Zarga sank down, and huddled with her face upon the floor. The butte was split in twain from summit to foundation, and tumbled in awful ruin to right and left. In the ragged jaws of the cleft stood the snow white figure of Lamara.

CHAPTER XIX
HOME THOUGHTS

THE genius of the Torides had qualities which more affiliated them with the people of our own earth than did that of the Saturnians. Their desire for power had stimulated them to develop the material sciences, and to experiment with a view to the physical control of nature for personal ends; whereas the Saturnians sought knowledge for the sake of its inherent goodness and beauty, and therefore aimed to obliterate self as far as they might, in order to thus remove the obstruction to influx and render themselves obedient channels of the omnipotent force. They used no writing, because such records of the past as were spiritually useful were spontaneously present with them in each passing hour, and the source of their wisdom constantly supplied them to the limits of their capacity; they built no enduring structures, because they could immediately fashion their natural surroundings into the form of their thoughts; they gave no labor to food and protection, because the substances necessary to their bodily nourishment passed into them in measure as waste created the demand, on a principle analogous to the flow of vegetable sap; and for defense, should that be required, they could so modify the vibrations of reflected light as to render themselves invisible. They were wholly occupied with the concerns of the moment; and they were independent of space, by reason of their ability not only to appear and to act at a distance mentally, but also to effect almost immediate bodily transference. The general result of all this was, not a complicated but an extremely simple manner of existence on the physical plane, interrupted on special occasions only for some exceptional purpose; their ordinary life was as artless and naïve as that of children; and they enriched their environment not otherwise than by establishing an increasing harmony between it and themselves. To this harmony was due the extension of their physical life to periods vastly beyond any imaginable limits of ours, accompanied throughout by a perfection of vigor and freshness which we ascribe to the prime of youth alone.

Widely alien from this, and more consonant with ours, were the methods and ambitions of the Torides, a self-centered and arrogant race, eager to amaze and subdue by arbitrary force, and far more conversant than are we not only with the more legitimate processes of science, but with those devices to effect illusion of sense and mental bewilderment and subjection which were practised to a limited degree by the necromancers and adepts of former ages. They were of a turbulent and restless temper, capable of daring and arduous enterprises, but always unsatisfied and unruly. Their present ruler exercised a sway over them more absolute and severe than any they had known for a long time; he possessed in the fullest degree the qualities of the Torides nature, supplemented by an intellectual training and accomplishment rivaled by no other. By means at his disposal he had acquainted himself with many details of the nature and civilization of most of the inhabitants of the planets of our system, and of our own earth especially; with the ultimate object, never yet avowed but intensely fostered, of obtaining supreme domination over them all. He had long been collecting the materials for achieving this stupendous project; and at the time of Miriam's arrival on the scene he conceived himself to be nearly ready to attempt it. The passion for possession of her which had seized upon him appeared to him to be something far above the limitations of a personal desire to enjoy her love and beauty; he imagined that a union with her would greatly enhance his chances of success in his cosmic adventure. Working together for that end, each would multiply the other's powers; and his actual contact with her, brief though it had been, and hostile outwardly, had confirmed his confidence in the final outcome.

Among his many studies he had not neglected research into the nature of woman, and fancied himself no tyro in that far-reaching and ramifying mystery. Miriam's unexampled exile from her home and people would render her, he reflected, tenderly susceptible to influences that should seem to conciliate that estrangement, and to make her forget the violence and extraordinary circumstances of her seizure, and he took his measures accordingly.

After conducting her into the castle he waved aside the guards and attendants who assembled to do them honor, and led her through several halls and antechambers, massively built and furnished with austere dignity, to an upper floor where a corridor opened before them wainscoted with light-tinted and polished woods, the upper walls and ceilings colored in cheerful hues, with designs gracefully and tastefully conceived. At the end of the passage he flung open a door, and stood aside, with an obeisance, for her to enter.

Upon crossing the threshold she found herself in the outermost of a suite of rooms, the first glimpse of which almost betrayed her into an exclamation of astonishment. He was watching her closely and he smiled.

"Anything you wish is at your service here," he said quietly. "There are women at your call to wait upon you. You are mistress of this place and of this planet. If you should be disposed to see me I will come; otherwise your privacy will be inviolate."

The door closed and she heard his tread departing down the passage.

After standing for a few moments, looking interestedly about her, while the stern expression of her face gradually softened with pleased surprise, she walked slowly through the five or six rooms of the apartment. At every step some new object aroused her wonder and gratification. If this were magic it was admirable employed!

The site was a replica, apparently exact, of her own rooms in her father's house on the Long Island shore. Had skilled architects and upholsterers employed months in executing a careful reproduction their success could not have been greater than had been here achieved, as it seemed, instantaneously. It was home itself! Even familiar trifles—an inlaid hand-mirror, an ivory fan from Burma, a silver flask of Damascus perfume, a color photograph of her father—were in their accustomed places. The rugs on the inlaid floors were of her own selection; the embroidery on the silken bed-covering was of her own design. Entering the room on the left of the bedchamber, which she had had fitted up as a study and laboratory, she found all her paraphernalia apparently as she had left them when going on her last visit to Mary Faust. This discovery aroused in her something more than surprise. She examined various articles minutely; then, throwing herself into the study chair, she spent some time in grave meditation. If this apparatus were as genuine as it looked, Torpeon had, no doubt, unwittingly put in her hands potent means for defeating his own plans. Before leaving her earth she had nearly completed an invention, based upon atomic disintegration, which was capable of being applied in a manner to give unexpected significance to his statement that she was "mistress of Tor." If the result of her experiments answered their promise the words would become something more than an empty compliment.

"At any rate," she told herself, "science is science, in one part of the universe as much as in another. But, of course, all this wonderful reproduction is a clever device to put me off my guard—an expansion of the same principle used by Hindu jugglers to beguile the senses. I seem to be at home again, but I am a prisoner here, nevertheless; and probably under constant observation. If there were only some one here whom I could trust!"

As she uttered the wish an incongruous thought of the grotesque little cripple, Jim, slipped into her mind. It was one of those unaccountable vagaries which characterize memory. She had never given more than passing attention to him. The impression was probably due to the prevailing, if sometimes subconscious, presence of Jack in her reflections; the one would suggest the other. Jack! Where was he? What was he doing or planning? Doubtless he would attempt to follow her. Aided by the Saturnians—but would they aid him? And must not Torpeon have prepared for all such contingencies? Did not the very liberality with which he treated her indicate his conviction that he was safe from attack? Yes; she must not depend upon outside assistance. She must fight for herself!

But, once more, that impression of the cripple returned to her. She half resented it. But she dismissed that feeling; the poor little creature could not be responsible for the notion. It was odd how clearly he was presented before her mind's eye. She must have taken more exact note of him than she had supposed. Jim was the only one of the three who had undergone no outward alteration on his arrival on Saturn; the flame garments which she and Jack had assumed had not replaced, for him, the quaint, terrestrial jacket and trousers which he had worn in New York. Jim was too elementary in his simplicity to undergo change. And yet the soul of him, which was loyal, honest and affectionate, must be capable, like all true and loving souls of indefinite development. But he would always be Jim! Miriam smiled and sighed. Then she rose, with an impatient impulse, and returned to the bedroom.

Yonder was her dressing-table in the corner, with the cheval-glass standing beside it, inclined at the angle she had last given it. She walked up to it with a feminine curiosity, to see how she looked in Saturnian costume.

She was frankly startled when the reflection given back to her showed her to be wearing the same dove-colored flying-suit that was her usual dress when visiting the Long Island estate. The degree of pleasure which this gave her was perhaps not logically justifiable. It seemed to bring her real home nearer than had any of the other features of the production of her familiar surroundings—reproduction, illusion, or whatever it might be. Here she stood, as she was accustomed to see herself! It restored her self-possession. And she yielded to a genuine emotion of gratitude to Torpeon, whose foresight must have been something more than self-interested to inspire him to such a thought. It implied real interest in her.

"The creature does really care for me!" she said to herself.

She seated herself in the chair before the dressing-table, and by the mere force of habit touched the bell-punch in the panel, by which she was wont to summon her personal maid, Jenny. Jenny was a New England girl, daughter of a farmer, who had been a chum of Terence Mayne before they emigrated to America. Old Mike, dying a widower in narrow circumstances, had left his daughter an orphan, and Terence, for old sake's sake, had brought her to New York to be Miriam's confidential attendant.

"Dear little Jenny!" murmured Miriam, as she sent the signal along the wire. "I wonder if she misses me! What kind of substitute will I get, do you suppose?"

The door leading into the servant's quarters opened quietly, and a light step was audible approaching from behind; that was how Jenny used to come in, and the rhythm of the steps was like hers. In a moment Jenny herself stood before her mistress and dropped a curtsy with her warm Hibernian smile.

"Did you ring, miss?" The well remembered lilt of the Cork brogue—Jenny was born in Old Kinsale!

"Bring me a cup of tea, Jenny," said Miriam. But this was mere reflex action, she had been too much amazed to express her amazement.

"Sure I will, miss, with pleasure," Jenny relied; and turned briskly and walked out. There had been no illusion about it, no reproduction. Inanimate things might be imitated, but not a human being in flesh and blood.

Miriam had leisure before Jenny returned with the tea-things on the tray to recover her breath and to turn the matter over in her mind. But the only result of her reflections was an increased admiration for Torpeon: a being who could do this was not to be despised. It showed something more and better than control of hidden agencies; there was a grace, a delicacy, in the achievement—a manifestation of the heart—which carried still further the kindly sentiment which she had begun to feel for him, in spite of her resolve to bring his purposes to naught

Now she heard the clink of the tea-things on the tray, and here was Jenny again, bearing the smoking teapot, the sugar, the sliced lemon, the thin slices of brown bread and butter, and the Japanese porcelain teacup and saucer.

CHAPTER XX
REBELLION

TORPEON, sitting alone in his official chamber, leaned his elbow on the table, his chin supported on his clenched fist, and bent his thoughts upon the problems before him.

His rule, despotic though it was, had never been free from difficulties. There were two parties among the Torides—one occupying the savage portion of the globe; the other the enlightened or civilized regions. Among the former were many outlaws—men who had either committed crimes against the state and had escaped from punishment; and also persons who had sacrificed such comforts as civilization afforded by reason of their dissatisfaction with the restrictions of a tyrannous government. Not a few of these were men of powerful and trained minds, resentful of interference with their freedom, and only needing an acknowledged leader and trustworthy organization to revolt. But they were jealous of one another, and the bulk of the population around them was hardly more amenable to discipline than so many wild beasts; the fugitive criminals, because of their innate and incorrigible wickedness, and the rest, because of their ignorance and semi-bestial condition. On our own planet spaces of thousands of centuries separate the cave men from the educated; but on Tor, the two lived side by side.

The physical environment on the dark side of Tor was terrific. The satellite, like our own moon, turned but one face to the sun, and though light was more diffused than with us, a twilight gloom reigned on the further side, alleviated only by outbursts of volcanic fires and by the electrical phenomena of gigantic storms. The surface was rocky, gashed with abysses and jagged with huge crags; caldrons of molten lava alternated with steaming or frozen lakes; and torrents of scalding water, hurled upward through subterranean passages in the crust of the globe, fell in headlong cascades, and fled away in boiling rivers through mountain ravines. Vegetation was scant and harsh: thorny trailers as thick as a man's leg crawled and twisted to vast distances from the crevices of the rocks, carrying poison in their thorns; and the dark leaves and juices of other plants were hostile to life and health. The only approach to a domestic animal was a genus of goats, fierce and agile, with menacing horns and bristly hides, which were snared and tethered, but not tamed, by the human inhabitants, for the sake of their milk and skins. Their flesh was boiled or steamed for food. Serpents, lizards and amorphous reptiles unknown to our fossil deposits inhabited the caves and clambered over the cliffs and gullies, shunning such dim light as there was, but lying in wait for incautious travelers. A kind of tiger, covered with shaggy red hair, and another beast kindred to the hyena, but as large as a horse and of a ghastly white hue, were the chief representatives of the feline and protelidae families. The hunting of these creatures, with blow-pipes and slings hurling sharp-cornered lumps of poisonous stone, was the main occupation of the more savage cave-dwellers. Their fur was plaited into a sort of garment.

People of this type were indigenous to the dark regions, and were under some degree of subjection to the outlaws of the civilized side. But no systematic effort to improve them had ever been made—they were the unwilling slaves of unloving masters. The more thoughtful of the latter had, indeed, sometimes considered the possibility of forming them into some sort of army, to attack Torpeon's domains; but the obstacles had proved insurmountable. Yet Torpeon had never felt secure.

His portion of the planet faced Saturn and the sun, and received a species of magnetic currents from the ring. Its topography was rugged and moderately fertile; five rivers from the Dark Mountains flowed down into an inland sea of bitter waters. The pastures were browsed by deerlike animals with smooth, straight horns. The most valuable domestic animals were a species of aquatic bird of the duck type, but larger than our condors; they existed in immense flocks and were very prolific. A leguminous plant was cultivated, allied to our beans, but of the size of a potato, and having the taste and some of the qualities of meat; when immature they could be ground into flour from which a rich and succulent bread was made. But to these staples science had added many viands concocted from inorganic substances, which could be rendered attractive to taste and sight by arts of the magical order.

The women of the Torides were taller and heavier than the men, but indolent and of inferior mentality; they were of domestic utility, but did not form a part of society; when mated, they would give birth to not more than two children each; there were no marriage laws, but a woman who had lived with a man might not afterward take another partner. As the sexes were about equally divided, the population remained stationary, and the relations were practically monogamic. Girls were bred to household employments; boys were drastically disciplined and educated by the state, both physically and mentally, and those who showed aptitude were initiated in science and magic.

Torpeon had assumed the chieftainship of this people by hereditary right; but he had soon manifested more than hereditary ability and force. He was profound in the lore of the masters, daring in speculation, arbitrary and resolute in will. He reduced his subjects to a uniform political level; there were no gradations between him and them. He made use, as he saw fit, of the brains and of the bodies of all, but shared his secrets with none. He had no commerce with women; but his vision extended far, and he knew of Miriam's journey and enough of her own character and quality to make him resolve upon their union. With and through her his dreams might be realized, and she might be safely admitted to his inmost aims and counsels.

Having succeeded in transporting her to his own abode, he meant to lose no time in putting his great scheme into operation. Some details of it were still unsettled; but there were reasons why a degree of risk must be faced in order to avoid other contingencies. Moreover, his wooing of Miriam—if it could be so termed—might prosper better after his main undertaking had been launched. The astounding achievement which he contemplated, by capturing her imagination, might lead the way to the surrender of her heart. She could not but love unexampled daring and irresistible power, even were there nothing else in him to attract her.

The most learned and efficient scientists in his kingdom had all been set to work to prepare the preliminaries for his grand coup; but to none had been confided the scope of the plan in its entirety—which was thus rendered secure from treasonable checks and interference. Cooperation in carrying out the various parts of the program was indispensable; but he alone—and, should it seem at the last moment desirable, Miriam—could know the end aimed at, and the manner in which it was to be attained.

There was the possibility of failure—that he realized; it would involve consequences so appalling, not only to Tor and its inhabitants, but to the solar system as a whole, that even Torpeon could not estimate them. On the other hand, there was the probability of success: he chose to fix his mind on that, and the thought exalted him almost to the level of deityship. The hazard was worth taking!

On the panel in front of him was a pentagonal plate of metal, furnished with figures and signs, arranged in a certain mutual relation and order, by means of which he was able to communicate with each of his scientific departments, and to determine, at a glance, how the work at any point was progressing. The hands on a score or more of small dials, arranged along the outer margins of the plate, registered the approximations of the several laboratory workers toward the completion of their assignments. All seemed to be proceeding smoothly—or all but one, Number Five, which was a trifle tardy and irregular in its movements. After observing this dial for awhile Torpeon put himself in touch with the operator.

"You are behind your schedule—why?"

A voice from the annunciator replied: "A counter current from Saturn; another from a source I have not determined. I am investigating."

"Report if interruptions continue; but make no attempt to prevent them without consulting me. If they abate, continue as before."

"Understand!" came the reply, and Torpeon leaned back in his chair.

"Number Five!" he muttered. He took a diagram from the table and studied it closely. "If Lamara suspects she would be more apt to attack Seven, or Nineteen. As for the 'other' source, that may be merely an echo. Or there may be some local disturbance; if so, it would prove temporary." He glanced again at the dial. "Ah, he has resumed! A false alarm. I will have a test made, nevertheless."

The matter did not seem urgent, however, and he put it aside for the moment. He rose and paced up and down the room with folded arms.

"What a voyage!" he said to himself, with the secret enthusiasm of a great adventurer. "There have been other conquerors; but none before me has conceived a campaign such as this! There have been mighty war-chariots, but none like mine! There have been wise men, but none till now has dared to loosen the anchors that hold the globes to their stations! All have been slaves to the laws assumed to be immutable. I have solved the secret of these invisible tethers and woven new ones of my own. I shall show that a man may be master of the universe. Day and night, heat and cold, seed time and harvest, shall come and go as I will. The sun himself shall do my bidding; and the vapors out of which worlds are made shall congeal or disperse at my pleasure. There have been heroes and kings; but I shall be the first of men to be acknowledged as a god and to breathe the air of immortality!

"But my victory would be barren," he continued, halting in his walk and stretching out his arms, "if it had to be enjoyed alone! For this reason have I till now only played with the great idea, instead of putting it to the proof. An Everlasting of loneliness would have been a dungeon of intolerable light! I saw it and I shrank from it. Seeking through the worlds I found none fit to share an adventure with me till now! But she is my companion of eternity; fate and circumstance, the dead drag of matter, could not keep us apart. And it was no blind chance that united us. The sources of the rivers of her being and mine were remote from each other, small and feeble; but within them was the hidden force which turned their flow to the point of meeting; they gathered strength as they proceeded; their tide was irresistible; they penetrated the mountains, they flooded the gulfs, space could not stay them; even the illusions of false persuasions fought against them in vain; and she is here! And her coming is the symbol and assurance that the circle shall be completed, and that I have not dreamed and wrought in vain!

"Miriam, my mate! Be proud and reluctant as you will; I love you but the more, and the fire of your love will burn only the clearer and more intensely when the error that confuses you has been burned away. You and I shall sit at our ease and smile at each other as we behold the phantasmagory of Creation pass in review at our feet! The great stars shall wither and crumble into dust, and we will arise in the freshness of our youth and summon others to bloom before us in the glory of their prime. The comets, as they pass, shall bring us tidings from afar, and bear our commands to regions yet unborn. Hand in hand we will pace through the avenues of infinity and determine the epochs of eternity with a kiss!"

In the midst of the room a small sphere of white light appeared and passed successively into yellow, green, rose, and purple. It disappeared slowly.

"Already, Miriam!" he exclaimed with a proud and joyful look; and catching up a scarlet mantle he opened the door and passed out.

CHAPTER XXI
CAVE MEN

KROTOX and Asgar had killed a goat and were eating it. They squatted at the entrance of their habitation, with the skinned carcass between them, and cut strips of flesh from it with their sharp stone knives. These they toasted over the red flames that flickered up from a crevice in the rocky platform which was their feeding place. Their cave was half-way up the side of a crag, at whose foot, several hundred feet below, ran a hot river from the lake that filled the basin further up the gorge. The path to the cave was a narrow footway formed partly by zigzag cracks in the face of the cliff, and partly of steps or holes made by hand. It was secure even from the big serpents and lizards, but not convenient for ordinary household purposes.

"You forgot the salt. It was your turn to get it," remarked Krotox.

"I had enough to do, killing the goat," returned Asgar. "You were down in the gorge and might have fetched up salt enough for a month from the pocket beside the basin. You'd like to doze here and let me run about and wait on you, I suppose!"

Krotox cracked a marrowbone between his jaws. "I had important business," he said. "You remember Yolgu? Well, he came over from the other side to-day."

"I didn't think he had the spirit for it," remarked Asgar. "Of course, he's planning to raise and army and capture Torpeon!" he added with a sneer.

"I didn't ask him. But he brought news."

The conversation was interrupted by a deep rumbling noise which caused the solid cliff to vibrate and the flame to leap up in the aperture. It was followed by an explosion in the group of mountains over against that on which they were, and a column of smoke and fire climbed heavily into the sky, spread out fountain-wise, and subsided, sending fragments of molten stone and cinders in all directions, some of them falling close to the entrance of the cave, into which Krotox and Asgar had withdrawn. They now resumed their places and their meal, letting the incident, which was far from being a novelty, pass without comment.

"News, eh?" grunted Asgar. "Another raid on Saturn, probably?"

"I said news!" retorted the other. "He has taken a woman!"

"Who? Yolgu?"

"No; Torpeon!"

"Torpeon! I wish I could believe it! When Torpeon takes a woman honest men may hope for their rights! But Yolgu was always a liar."

"And Asgar will never cease being a fool. Torpeon has taken a woman, and he got her from the little planet down beyond Jupiter."

Asgar chuckled contemptuously. "Did she bring her little planet with her?"

"She was visiting Lamara," Krotox continued composedly. "There were details, but nothing of importance. Torpeon got her away, and she is now with him at the castle. Yolgu saw her just before he came here. She's not like our kind, or the Saturnians either."

Asgar meditated for a while. "Even if the story were true," he said at last, "I don't see how it would help us."

"I was waiting for you to say that!" observed Krotox with a sardonic glance. "In the first place, she's a woman; next, she has new magic; thirdly, she came unwillingly. The result is certain! But not so certain as that you are going to ask me how?"

"I question only persons capable of intelligent answers," rejoined the other. "You spoke of the details of her coming as being unimportant; to my mind they are quite as important as her arrival itself. Whether she came alone; if not, who were her companions; whether she gained access to Saturn through Lamara's help or independently; what object had she proposed to herself: points such as these might enable us to judge whether the situation warranted our concerning ourselves about the matter. But—"

At this juncture there was another interruption. Though by no means as outrageous and cataclysmic as the other, it produced a much more startling effect on the two troglodytes. They threw themselves flat on their stomachs and peered cautiously over the edge of the rocky shelf. The sound had come from below. The custom of social visiting had never been in vogue on the dark side of Tor, and any invasion of privacy was likely to suggest a hostile intent. "Where are the poison-stones?" whispered Asgar.

"I have three here," replied Krotox, "but I won't waste them on you—you couldn't hit the earth from the top of a pock tree! I see nothing: it must have been a tiger."

"It was more like a hyena—hark!"

A peculiar call again sounded from below. "Coo-ee!"

The men exchanged an uneasy look, but remained silent. The gorge was deep, and wreaths of smoke from the volcano, yellow and sluggish, were coiling through it."

"Hello, you dubs!" presently came a shrill voice out of the abyss. "Ain't yer got no elevator in dis joint? Does yer haul yer patrons up wid a rope? Well, I's a comin', anyway; so stick de ham-an'-eggs inter de saucepan an' a go uv lager on de side! I's bringin' me hunger wid me!"

"I see it now!" whispered Asgar; "give me a stone—ah, you missed it! What is it—a goblin? It climbs like a beetle!"

Krotox hurled another stone.

"You guys ain't even in de class uv de bush-leaguers," remarked the voice, sounding nearer than before, and in no way discouraged by this reception. "Never seen my spit-ball, did yer? Say, she curves roun' de batter's nut and swats him in de off eye! Ef dat's yer best yer goes back to de bench. Git me?"

"It's coming straight up the cliff!" exclaimed Krotox in dismay. "It must be a goblin! I never saw one before; we must pretend we're glad to see it!"

"Get if off its guard and then leave it to me," muttered Asgar. "It'll go down faster than it came up!"

This hospitable purpose had no sooner been formulated than the visitor's head appeared above the level of the ledge, and the next moment he was standing beside the remnants of the goat; a one-legged apparition, supported under his left shoulder by a black crutch. His involuntary hosts regarded him with grimaces of feigned welcome, which ill disguised their fear and amazement. They were crouching on their hams at the mouth of the cavern.

"Home-sweet-home!" called out the apparition cheerfully; he was not even winded by his extraordinary feat. "Git up an' hustle now, you ginks; yer ain't in de habit uv meetin' toffs like me—I kin see dat! So dis is de roof-gard'n; eh? Don' bodder wid de cabbyrat stuff—my time's wort' about ten plunks an inch, an' dirt cheap at dat! I's de One-Legged Avenger, an' I's campin' on de trail uv ol' Torpy! Has eeder o' you ducks seen him—dat fuzzy-haired geezer wid de red sweater looped round him? Cough up!"

Jim's dialect was doubtless modified to Toridian ears by planetary conditions; but it was Krotox, who was bony, aquiline, and quicker of apprehension than his lethargic and unwieldy companion, who was first able to decipher the code: for "Torpy" read "Torpeon."

"The person you mention, worshipful stranger," he said in his most sugary accents, "does not rule over this side of our planet, and is never seen here. To find him, you must travel east, passing those two ranges of mountains, by way of that volcano which is just now beginning an eruption. Beyond that is a lake, which—"

"Yer kin bite it off right dere, ol' pal," interposed Jim; "I ain't in de g'ography class dis trip. Git me headed right an' I'm dere—see? Me an' Torpy has a bone to pick togedder, an' I'm treatin' some ginks ter a feed at Delmonniker's at eight-t'irty, an' me wid about a billion miles ter cover between dis and dat; so I ain't loafin' on me job. I'll mebbe be back later an' give t'ings here de once-over. Looks like dere might be a boom in real-estate in dese parts. Got a ticker inside? What's de quotin's on city lots in dis block? Gimme de inside an' den some? I ain't no piker!"

Krotox and Asgar looked at each other in manifest perplexity. Though not unfamiliar with trouble, some of our modern afflictions were still unknown to them. But they were interested in the allusions to Torpeon; if this supernatural creature had hostile designs against the common enemy the opportunity should be improved.

"Powerful being," said Asgar, "we are poor exiles and know nothing of the things you speak of, whether they be animals or vegetables. But Torpeon is the author of our misfortunes, and if he has also wronged you, we may be of use to one another."

"Now yer talkin', an' we gits down to brass tacks," Jim replied with animation. "Dis geezer has swiped de gal uv a frien' o' mine; an' me, I's figgerin' to counter on his jaw an' do de reskoo stunt—see? Ef you ducks has de inside track mapped out, gimme de tip; an' when I lan's de goods, I take de gal, an' what's left yer stuffs in yer jeans an' dey won' be no come-back on it. Mebbe," he added thoughtfully, "me line o' talk is some too illegint fer de likes o' you poor hoboes; but I's doin' me best!"

"If your grace condescends to extend protection over us, we are the slaves of your will," rejoined Asgar, after he and Krotox had conferred for a few moments. "It is known to us that the sinful Torpeon has done this crowning outrage, and plans others, unless prevented. If you will graciously kill him you shall be king of all our country, and we, your ministers, will lay its spoils and its inhabitants at your feet."

"Lil ol' N'York is good enough for me, but I reco'nizes yer obligin' sperrit," said Jim agreeably. "We plays de Evans's gambit, an' I figgers to checkmate de black king in four moves. Dere'll be glory enough fer all, an' yer takes de rinsin's a free gift. Ef dat's a go, put it dere!"

He extended his hand, which Asgar and Krotox in succession humbly touched to their foreheads.

"Now kids," Jim proceeded, "yer sees dis here kyar!" He exhibited his crutch, patting it caressingly as if it were a beautiful vehicle of the most luxurious and costly description. "We gets aboard, an' we steers due east till we sights de stronghold uv de inimy. Nobody don't see us—'cause why?—I turns de peg here in de neck an' crack!—we vanishes like blowin' out de gas in de hotel room-wid-bat'. I mounts de secret back stairs, an' fust t'ing yer knows yer sees Torpy flyin' out de top-story winder an' lightin' on his nut. Dat's the signal fer startin' 'Hail to der Chief,' an' me and de lady appears on de battlemints, an' waves our han's gracious to der applaudin' t'ousands. Dere's mebbe some t'ings I's left out o' de yarn; but yer gits me drift! All you gotta do is yank off yer shirt an' holler yer heads off, while me and de lady sings 'Good-by, proud worl', we's goin' home,' de lights shets off an' we sinks below de verge ter show music. Are yer on?"

"Mighty emperor, dispose of us as you will!" grunted Asgar and Krotox, bewildered into hypnosis by this rousing exhortation.

"Git astride de stick an' come on!" Jim ordered; and the monstrous ravines and peaks of Tor sank beneath them.

CHAPTER XXII
MIRIAM

"SURE, miss," Jenny allowed herself to say, as she set down the tea-tray before her mistress, "'tis a sight for sore eyes ye are! You seeming so natural-like, after all the signs and wonders. And the rooms and all just the same! However did it happen I don't know. Up till you touched the bell, I says to meself, 'Jenny, ye're dreaming!'"

"A great poet said, 'The earth hath bubbles, as the water hath, and these are of them,'" replied Miriam. "Nobody really knows the difference between what seems and what is. We may be content if they seem as we would wish to have them. But I suppose you know how you got here?"

"'Deed, miss, and I don't, then! I'd been sorrowing that ye weren't at home these last days, and the poor master taking on so; and last evening, I think it was, I was saying me prayers, and, of a sudden, 'What's that?' I says. Whether I saw it or I heard it, I couldn't rightly tell, miss, but somebody was in the room; and what did I do but shut my eyes so as I'd see better—if ye understand how I mean, miss. And there was a lady there—fine and stately she was, but not the blessed Mary, for she had on black in place of white, and no glory round her head; but oh, 'twas the face of somebody great and good, I'll go bail for that! And whether she spoke or not I don't know; but seems like I knew what was in her mind—all calmness and kindness, and 'Don't be afeared, Jenny, ye're in friendly hands'—it came to me like that. And it seemed like I wasn't to open my eyes, but leave it all to her; a kind of lullaby like, miss, the way my mother—God rest her soul—would sing me asleep when I was a wee colleen, back in the ould sod.

"'Sure,' says I to meself, 'it's dying I am,' I says; it was a sort of drawing out through the top of me head, but soft and gentle, and me not a bit frighted, but easy and pleased like never before in all me life; and the next minute what did I see but meself sitting there in the rocker, and meself standing beside her—if you understand me, miss. 'If I'm dead,' I says, 'however would I be alive?' I says; and with that I looks round and sees you your own self, miss, but oh, ever and ever so far off—standing here by the table, you were, and a thoughtful and sad look on the sweet face of ye. 'Sure, 'tis going to her I'll be,' I says, forgetting the distance; but the wish in me was like wings, and me like outside meself. Howandever, going I was, not like flying, but what was before me one minute was behind me in another, with me standing still all the time and the things moving past me. 'Sure,' I says to meself, 'Jenny,' I says, 'ye'll never see yourself again,' I says, thinking of meself sitting there in the rocker. But I'll be talking too much miss," said Jenny, interrupting herself and handing her mistress the napkin.

Jenny's voice had the flow and modulations of bubbling waters and singing birds, and it was no hardship to listen to her even on ordinary topics.

"It's a wonderful story, Jenny," Miriam said. "Wishes, after all, are the greatest power in the world; they are in science and art and deeds, like the soul in the body. But time and space, like veils, keep us from recognizing the miracle of it. But sometimes the veils may be lifted, and then we see. I'm glad you are here."

"So am I, miss," returned Jenny. "But how will we be getting back again?"

"By wishing, perhaps," said Miriam, with a smile. "But we'll have to help ourselves a little, too, I think. So it was Mary Faust, after all," she said to herself; "but she must have somehow cooperated with Torpeon. Lamara, also, perhaps. Oh, I hope Jack does nothing rash! But I must do my part! Is any one beside yourself here, Jenny?"

"'Tis that puzzles me, miss," answered the girl. "Times I'll be wanting something, and looks round; there it sits, like it had been there all the time, but never a body have I seen to bring it. 'Tis a queer place entirely! More like dreams than any living place I know of. Sure I'm wondering, now and again, will I wake up of a sudden and find meself asleep!"

"I have felt that in other places before this," said Miriam. "But if you can get what you want by wanting it, perhaps I can do the same. You may take back the things; the tea tasted very good."

"I found the tea in the caddy, miss, but I made it meself," said Jenny, showing her milk-white teeth between her red lips; and she departed with the tray.

Miriam leaned her head on her hand and remained quiescent for a while. Presently she loosened the fastenings of her hair, and let the magnificent flood of it tumble down past her shoulders to her flanks. She took a brush and began to brush it with long, sweeping movements. As the delicate silken filaments responded to the treatment with increased softness and luster, her mind became composed, and her thoughts clear and orderly. In times past she had solved many a problem with a hair-brush.

She looped the great, black strands round her wrist, and by some feminine sleight of hand caused it to coil itself upon her head; her supple fingers pierced the mounded mass with fairy poinards and lightly patted it into symmetry. She contemplated the effect in the glass with approval; but the red mark of Torpeon caused a frown to flit over her brow.

The suggestion conveyed by Jenny's story that Mary Faust might have had some share at least in the preparation of her present surroundings had opened the way to fresh thoughts and hopes. It somewhat modified her view of Torpeon's chivalric initiative, though she could still concede him whatever credit was due to his accepting a happy proposal. It was out of the question, of course, that he and Mary Faust could have in view the same ultimate objects; but Mary's was the deeper nature, and doubtless the profounder science, and she might have led him to play unawares into her hands. She rose and went into the laboratory.

Miriam selected from the instruments on the table a small machine with a four-sided crystal cup at one end and a retort at the other; these were connected by metal parts which included two balls a third of an inch in diameter, which ran up and down in grooves that were tipped rhythmically to right and left by the action of fine-toothed gear; a closely coiled gold wire connected the cup and the retort, and yielded to the stress applied and relaxed by the seesaw movement of the grooved shafts. The whole contrivance was embraced in a magnetic field created by a bar of iron alloyed with another metal isolated by Miriam herself, bent into the form of a horseshoe.

She uncorked a vial containing a transparent but very heavy liquid, colorless and sparling, and carefully counted seventeen drops of it into the crystal cup. As it fell, it had the peculiar consistency of quicksilver; but the drops immediately resolved themselves into a homogeneous mass. She next armed herself with a delicate pair of pincers, and with them picked out a grain of what looked like black powder from a box partly filled with them. She dropped this grain into the cup of liquid.

For a moment it lay of the surface, causing a slight depression to appear beneath it, a miniature dimple. Then it seemed to be attacked by the liquid, which was seen to gyrate around it from left to right, and this movement spread until the entire surface was agitated. The black particle first became red, like heated iron, and finally burned with a clear flame until it was wholly consumed; the liquid meanwhile becoming clouded, but finally assumed a brilliant blue color. At the same time, there appeared in the retort two small globes of fire, intensely bright, which revolved round each other with gradually increasing speed.

When the rapidity of their motion had caused them to take the aspect of a ring, Miriam nodded to herself with murmur of satisfaction, lifted back the magnet, and the flames vanished, the gyration of the liquid ceased, and the experiment was over.

"Everything seems right," she said to herself. "I have only to reverse the circuit, and it is done! But Torpeon must be either very ignorant or very confident to allow me access to these things. Or he may imagine they are mere toys that I amuse myself with. He is himself planning something—I feel sure of that! Perhaps, after all," she went on after a pause, "Mary Faust has more control over him than he suspects. She certainly knows my predicament. Why did she send no message by Jenny? Perhaps she thought her too simple to risk in these intrigues. But I need some one—some one that I can trust. Suppose Torpeon should put me where I could not get to my laboratory! If he were certain I would never yield to him, he might do anything! If I cannot find an assistant, I must devise some way of acting from a distance—and that might miscarry! Terrible, either way! But I must do my best! What if I should do it now!" she suddenly exclaimed aloud, rising to her feet, her cheeks paling and her eyes dark under the influence of a powerful emotion. Her hand crept toward the instrument and laid hold of the magnet. "This may be my last opportunity! Jack—Jack, my own darling, you will know I could never love any one but you!"

She had begun to turn the magnet back to its original position when she felt three light touches on her breast. Mary Faust's warning once more!

She had nerved herself to a desperate act, and the reaction caused by this admonition, with its reassuring implication, shook her to the soul.

She sank down in her chair, buried her face in her hands, and sobbed uncontrollably.

The paroxysm did not last long. She mastered herself with a feeling of self-contempt and sat up, wiping her eyes and pressing her cold hands against her hot cheeks.

"Yes, it was wicked and cowardly—God forgive me!" she said. "I am not brave; I must be prevented and led, like a spoiled child! Jack, I'm not worthy of you!"

She walked up and down the room, calming herself, her courage revived. She had not been abandoned; there would be some way out. The irrevocable deed she had contemplated could be at least postponed. Wiser and stronger spirits than hers were aware of her extremity, and were working for her.

"I will see Torpeon," she decided. "He must understand that, in spite of appearances, we are on equal ground."

She passed into the adjoining room, and was about to press the bell to summon Jenny, when that rosy-cheeked young woman knocked and opened the door.

"If you please, miss, a young man outside would like to speak with ye. He's a funny kind of young man, miss, if ye please," she added, breaking into a smile.

"How so, Jenny?" demanded Miriam. "Who sent him here?"

"He's from New York, miss, and I think he come of himself."

"From New York? Come of himself: Consider what you are saying, Jenny!" Then the thought of her lover leaped up in her. She seized the girl by the shoulders. "You don't mean—not Mr. Jack Paladin?"

Jenny was frightened by the passion in her look and voice.

"Oh, no, miss! I'm sorry, miss. It isn't that sort of gentlemen—just a young man, and he hasn't only one leg!"

Miriam dropped her arms with a heavy sigh. "Oh—Jim!" The intonation was not complimentary. Yet her face lightened up a little as Jim, with his indomitable grin, hobbled briskly into the room.

CHAPTER XXIII
TRUTH

LAMARA sat on a bench in the island garden, her hands folded in her lap. The bench was carved out of a piece of chalcedony, with soft orange-veins running through it, and bearing figures in high relief of little children tossing balls from one to another. The color was so adapted as to give the figures the hues of life; and if glanced at sidelong, one could fancy they had the movement and diversity of living beings. The bench was overshadowed by the level boughs of a tree, amid the dark, whispering leaves of which appeared globes of fruit that glowed and brightened as if by some innate quality; they were hidden intermittently as the breeze passed among them, and reappeared as buds, which blossomed and became fruit again. Wherever Lamara was, the fire of life seemed to be stimulated by the combined intensity and calm of her own being.

Up and down in the short pathway before her, Jack paced to and fro, restless as a high-strung horse galled by his tether. Lamara observed him with sympathy tinged with grave amusement.

He stooped before her at length, and resumed the conversation in which they had been engaged. "If it concerned only myself, it would be easy to be patient," he expostulated. "But when a man loves a woman, and she is in danger, you might as well expect him to be dead and alive at the same moment! If I could only so much as see her—but how can I tell what may be happening to her at this moment, and me good for nothing here! There can be no possible use for me in the world except to protect her. You have the means, and you won't give them to me! Why, even on my own earth I could use wings and weapons—and I ask nothing better! Argon is ready to help me if you give the word! But I don't want to interfere with your laws or customs; let me go alone, as I am, and meet this robber with my bare hands. I'm not a Saturnian, and you wouldn't be discredited by what I did. You got me out of that cave. Why should you stop there? Men where I come from have their own way of settling their quarrels, and I know no other! You've been kind to me, and I know how good and great you are; but it's cruelty to keep me here! If you would speak the word, I know I could be on Tor in a moment! What right have you to refuse it?"

"My poor boy, it is you, not I, that prevents all you wish," said Lamara gently.

"That's hardest of all to hear!" he exclaimed. "I'd die to save her! Could I do more? And you tell me I prevent myself!"

"You can do more than die—you can live and be yourself," she answered. "Sit beside me here for a little, Jack, and try to hear me."

He fetched a deep breath, took his place on the bench, folded his arms, and compressed his lips. She patted his broad shoulder in a sisterly fashion and went on:

"There is a sort of rite here, come down to us from old times. We didn't make it—it was given to us. When one of us has won the great victory, a halo appears over his head. It is the sign that he has entered into himself, and nothing can harm him afterward; and all nature is open to him and serves him."

"The great victory? Over what? Let me try! I ask no better!"

"No evil can prevail over one who has overcome the ally of evil in himself," said Lamara. "Dear Jack, no one, of himself, can really do anything. We see paradise before us, but we are kept from it by a wall, and we say we are shut out by some higher power. But the wall is ourselves, and we built it and placed it there. And not even the Spirit Himself, but only we ourselves, who raised it, can level it again and enter the divine garden."

"But you said we, of ourselves, can do nothing."

"Yes, and that is the truth! And yet it is the truth that we can do this, and when it is done we need do no more. All else is given to us freely."

Jack gazed perplexedly at her.

"If you look at the sun, you will see darkness; but it is light," she continued.

He shook his head despondently. "It's too deep for me!"

"There is nothing else deeper," she answered. "You know there is one God, and that He is life; and yet you see what you call life all round us—in these flowers and birds and the very earth, and in yourself; but if life be God, how can these things be alive, unless they are God? And you know they are not!"

"Can you tell me how?" he asked.

"I can tell you only that these things, you and I, are creatures which live and move by a life which is in them, and yet is not their own. And to be free to enter paradise, we must think life is our own, and act as if it were, and yet know that it is not. It is that knowing that is the great secret. For by that knowing, what is ourself is conquered and disappears, and the infinite self enters and fills its place. There are no more barriers or failures after that!"

"But that would mean that we are mere puppets, without freedom!"

"That is what wise men say," said Lamara, with a friendly smile; "but children know it is otherwise. They know the difference between puppets and creatures."

"I'm neither a child nor a wise man," said Jack unhappily.

"Perhaps you are nearer a child than you suspect," she rejoined. "You stand before the Third Gate, which is high and strong; but it opens at the right touch! If you were given power to overcome Torpeon, and to have Miriam for your own all your lives, but were told you must pay for it by seeing her a little less high and pure and happy than before, would you still take the power that was offered?"

After a pause: "No!" he said.

"Violence is evil, and evil in ourselves is the enemy's hold upon us," she rejoined.

"But Miriam has no thought of violence!"

"Have you not said that you and she were one? But come with me!"

She rose, and he followed her along the winding path to the pavilion, which they entered by a side door. It was the first time he had seen the interior. Nothing, however, was changed except for the fountain, which, instead of presenting a succession of figures, as before, now fell in a wide sheet of pure water, with a smooth and even surface. A slab of black marble, behind it, gave a deep tone to the water, like that of a dark, still pool. A white effervescence of foam, creating a pleasant murmur, was formed by the impact of the fall in the basin. Lamara motioned to her companion to take his place beside her on the seat in front of the fall.

"I come here to hold communication with our people," she remarked, "and sometimes with what lies beyond our own borders. Our planet is large, and has many inhabitants of many kinds, though all agree together; but they are divided, not into nations, as with you, but into societies, small or large, each composed of persons specially suited to one another. The societies, too, have their positions relative to one another, according to their functions and enlightenment, so that they can cooperate at need, as do the parts of our individual bodies. At such times they become mutually self-conscious; but in general, they are secluded in their proper boundaries or protected—even smaller groups or separate persons, if desired—by the veil of invisibility, which is our common heritage."

Jack had observed the apparent scantiness of population on this vast globe, which was now explained. "I wouldn't like to trust our people with such a faculty," he said frankly. "Nobody would feel safe!"

"Your people are traveling another route than ours," replied Lamara. "But they will reach and perhaps pass the degree in which we are. Among all the myriad myriads of worlds, no two are alike. You bear the burdens of many!"

"What an irresistible army you could raise!" he muttered. "You could conquer all the earths that surround the sun!"

Lamara laughed. "It would make me happier to help one man of another earth to conquer himself!" she answered. "But you may see an event which will show you, better than any words of mine, the fruit of such attempts and ambitions. But I didn't bring you here for that!"

She was silent, and Jack was obscurely conscious of a tension in the atmosphere, more subtle than that of electricity, which strung his mental faculties to a high pitch. His attention was involuntarily drawn to the fountain.

"You have been deceived by a false mirror," said Lamara; "now you shall be instructed by a true one. There is no magic here; the bending of the rays obeys a natural law. You will see the reflection of a reality which is taking place at this moment. But do not speak while it passes."

As she ceased, the darkness of the mirror became light, and there was painted upon it a fleeting stream of strange sights which Jack's eyes could not clearly interpret; the effect was as if they had leaped into space, and were passing through it with the speed of light. In a moment there had flashed across the surface the vision of an unimagined and formidable earth, ruddy and sinister; it was gone, and now appeared the interior of a room of severe but pleasing proportions, fitted with the tables and shelves of a laboratory. A woman sat at the table, with an instrument before her. She was in an attitude of deep meditation. Her face, as she sat thus, was fully revealed; but Jack had known her at the first glance. He made a sudden movement; but Lamara's hand on his arm reminded him of the injunction, and he was mute.

Through the silent mediumship of Lamara, however, he was able to read the thoughts that were passing through Miriam's mind as easily as he could discern her figure. He realized the potency of the machine, and followed the successive movements of her brain until her sudden resolve to reverse the magnet and precipitate the catastrophe. Her appeal to him at the supreme moment seemed to ring in his ears. He forgot everything except the overpowering impulse to arrest her hand, and he leaped to his feet with a passionate cry:

"No, no, beloved! Not that! Oh, God, protect her!"

The water mirror quivered, and was dissolved into broken strands of glittering spray. He staggered as he stood, staring wildly about him.

"The prayer was heard," spoke Lamara's tranquil voice. "But let her peril keep you mindful of your own! It is better for you as well as for her to trust in God than to the impious suggestion of your own heart!"

"A moment more and the whole globe on which she stood would have been shattered to atoms!" he groaned. "Oh, Miriam—Miriam!"

"Love is the greatest thing in the world," said Lamara; "but if, for the sake of that supreme good, you work evil against another fellow creature—if you summon the demon to save the angel—the demon triumphs and the angel is withdrawn."

"But to stand here helpless!" he groaned again, clenching his fists.

"No one is alone in the world; it may happen that a pygmy may succor a giant," she replied. But she did not interpret the apolog.

CHAPTER XXIV
THE HIGH COURT

AT a high point of the seacoast there lay a great amphitheater, the period of whose construction was known to none living; it had stood there for more than a thousand Saturnian generations; and there was a general belief that it was substantially a natural phenomenon, shaped out by unknown forces before the dawn of man, and added to or modified by human architects to adapt it more completely for its function. It possessed a mountainous grandeur and dignity, such as mortal hands might enhance, but not create.

The land sloped sharply toward the sea, and the amphitheater was delved out of the eastern face of the declivity. Its form was a complete oval; the benches, rank after rank, following the curve, only the eastward or seaward end of the vast sweep being left open. At the focus of the ellipse at this end was the raised level space used for a stage. The longer diameter of the structure may have been a thousand yards, and there was ample accommodation for a million persons. Dimensions so vast would have rendered the place useless for practical purposes on our planet, but offered no hindrance to the sight or hearing of a people endowed with the superior senses of the Saturnians.

It was the meeting-place of the people, who were summoned thither on occasions both of affairs of state and of entertainment or instruction. No one was barred from these sessions; but, as a rule, the population was present by deputies from each society. High courts of judgment were held here, but these had become rare, because social order was spontaneous and almost invariable in a community which had solved the problem of combining universal cooperation with gradations of rank.

At noon of the day following Lamara's interview with Jack, the amphitheater stood apparently empty. Row after row of vacant benches mounted skyward, the light and shadow making them look like finely etched lines in an innumerable series, divided by radiating divisions at right angles to the curve, defining to each society its appointed section. On the stage, facing the auditorium, were placed twelve chairs or thrones, one of which stood somewhat behind and above the others, which formed a semicircle. At the sides of the stage were several seats, to be occupied by persons having some subordinate share in the proceedings. Directly opposite the thrones was a single chair assigned to the individual to be tried; for this was to be a day of judgment. Between this chair and the judges stood an altar of black marble on which rested a piece of crystal fashioned into the shape of a heart.

A few minutes before noon Argon entered the theater at the stage end, accompanied by Jack. The young Saturnian led his friend to the chairs on the right, and they sat down. Jack cast a marveling look over the enormous interior, silent and tenantless; above bent the heavens, crossed by the arch of the ring, and with the moons set like gleaming jewels in the expanse. To the left, through the wide aperture of the entrance, lay the sea. The sun was near the zenith.

"Won't it take a long time to fill this space?" asked Jack. "We are the first here, and I saw no one in the neighborhood as we were on our way."

Argon, who was wearing a very grave look, roused himself and smiled.

"Our people are usually punctual, especially on such an occasion as this," he said. "You will see that we won't be kept waiting. I never thought," he added with a sigh, "to have come here on this errand! I've seen only joyful spectacles until now."

"You haven't told me what is to be done here," Jack observed. "Is it a criminal case? What penalties does your law inflict?"

"No Saturnian can inflict punishment on another!" answered Argon in surprise. "Our high courts do not convene for that purpose."

Jack was equally astonished. "What is their purpose, then?"

"To hear the charge and the answer of the accused."

"And is nothing done to the accused if found guilty?"

"Isn't it enough that the guilt should be fixed?"

"But what is to deter him from committing other crimes?"

"Such a thing never has been known," said Argon. "Could anything deter him more than to have his crime proved before the assembly of the people—to sit there with all eyes upon him and to go forth burdened by that shame? Those whom I have seen arraigned—and there have been very few in my lifetime—have become afterward more diligent and devoted than others in serving the common good. They have given no thought to their own comfort and welfare, but have made every sacrifice and effort to win back the approval of the community. Yes," he continued, "I remember learning that it is different with you. But with you there are sickness and struggle, and some, I've been told, are actually without means to live—though how that can be, when many of you have more than they need, I couldn't understand—and perhaps the statement was untrue. But, at any rate, you have temptations which we know nothing of here. All of us have more than all we need; there is no envy or hatred; each is content in the degree to which he belongs; each works at what he loves best to do, and does best, and he knows that the state needs him in his place, and that in any other he would be useless. So the temptation to do evil seldom is felt. Perhaps, if we had your troubles, we should have your crimes—and your punishments!"

There was a sound of trumpets; and Jack saw, in the center of the arena, three men who raised long, slender instruments to their lips and blew. As the sound died away, an amazing sight was revealed.

As if created by the musical notes, the entire array of benches lining the auditorium was filled from floor to parapet with men and women. A million human beings had suddenly sprung to life where, a moment before, there had seemed to be stark emptiness. Each of the innumerable societies, in its place, glittered in its flame-garments, tinted according to its quality and function in the state; and these were ranged in such a manner that their several characters, and even the individual variations of the persons composing them, could be perceived at a glance. The white societies occupied the benches immediately above the stage on each side;

the gold were next to them; the rose, the azure, and the violet followed in their order; and whether because of the brightness of the light everywhere diffused, or the translucency of the atmosphere, or because his eyes had acquired a power of vision hitherto unknown, Jack found himself able to discern with entire distinctness the forms and features of even the most distant members of that immeasurable assemblage. What beauty of women, what nobility of men, what grace and simplicity of demeanor, what frank and kindly looks! The true brotherhood of man was revealed in the splendor of its loveliness.

As he gazed, delighted and yet appalled, a recollection passed through his mind of the last great popular gathering that he had witnessed in his own world. How similar, and yet, in comparison, how paltry, confused, and obscure; and above all, how inferior in the spiritual influence that proceeded from it! There, there had been a heterogeneous multitude of individuals, each self-centered and scant in sympathy; here, the millionfold audience was like one incomparably gifted being—one mind, heart, and soul incarnated in innumerable male and female forms, various, inexhaustible, harmonious; mighty, powerful, beneficent. What might not such an organization, working for good, accomplish! And this audience was but a deputation from a race many thousand times as numerous and strong, and not less pledged to unity.

"You are right," Jack said to Argon, after contemplating the gathering. "No criminal would dare to face such a court more than once. But when shall we see the judges themselves and the accused?"

He had already perceived that the apparent simultaneous filling of the amphitheater had been due to the principle of voluntary invisibility and visibility which Lamara had explained to him. The spectators had probably been assembling for hours, but had waited to unveil until the trumpet sounded.

"We shall not have to wait long," replied his friend.

"Are you acquainted with the accused?" he asked.

"Yes—and you know her, also," Argon replied in a burdened voice.

"It's a woman, then?" exclaimed Jack, startled; but further words were prevented by the sounding of another signal by the trumpeters.

The silvery cadences filled the great oval cup with stately melody, and floated lingeringly away in the upper air.

"Look!" whispered Argon.

Beginning at either end of the arc of eleven thrones, the judges were, one after one, revealed in their places. Composed and serious they were as graven images of justice; but of a justice in which mercy bore an equal part. There was neither severity nor indifference in the expression of their countenances, but a meditative sadness, as if each were searching his own heart to detect there some trace of mortal frailty which should admonish him of his brotherhood with the most sinful.

The central figure, immediately below the higher throne, was Aunion. There was an expectant hush, and, like the slow dawning of a white light, the gracious form of Lamara appeared in her station above. Immediately the whole body of the audience rose in its places, and all silently lifted their right hands. She responded with a gesture of the arm, full of gentle majesty, which seemed to invoke love upon all.

The high court was open. Aunion was the first to speak.

"We are met," he said, "to hear the cause of one of us who has been charged with betraying a trust. The accused is a woman—young, as we measure age, and therefore to be thought of with the tenderness and indulgence which the inexperience of youth and the impulsiveness of girlhood may claim, and yet removed far enough from childhood to have lost something of the divine innocence and wisdom which children bring with them from the source of good. Had she been further advanced in the practise of self-government, we may believe that she would not stand accountant for this sin. It is likewise to be urged in her behalf that there flows in her veins blood of another strain than ours, which, even after the lapse of some ages, may abate her strength when and where it were most needed."

"On the other hand," he went on, "you are to know that the accused has been brought up in a position of exceptional advantage; she has been loved by our highest, and been admitted to the inner degrees of illumination. Moreover, her attempt was leveled not against one of ourselves, but against one of a race unfamiliar with our customs, and perhaps supplied with means less adequate than ours to offer resistance. The attempt failed, and you are to consider whether this fact relieves the accused in any degree from the odium of her purpose.

"To make an end, I say, that if any here can find nothing in his memory of his own secret life that would prompt him to show mercy to this girl, let him withdraw from our assembly, for that person is either more or less than human, and therefore not qualified to judge."

He ceased, and Lamara said: "Let the accused appear!" At the word the chair, hitherto the only one vacant in the amphitheater, was occupied by a slender figure, crouched forward, whose long golden hair, drawn before her face by her hands, confirmed the painful anticipation which Jack had already formed. After a moment the hands fell, and the face of Zarga was revealed. Jack was about to utter some protest, but Argon restrained him.

"Who accuses this girl?" asked Lamara.

Argon rose and stepped forward.

"I accuse her!" said he.

CHAPTER XXV
JUDGEMENT

PROBABLY none of the myriads who leaned forward to observe the proceedings, except Jack, were surprised at these words. He had not fathomed the nature of the Saturnians. He might have looked for the brother of the culprit to appear as her defender. But as her accuser—incredible!

Indeed, the entire conduct of the court thus far had been unimaginable, in his ideas of legal procedure. The chief judge had begun by stating in outline the crime of the accused, preceding it by what amounted to a plea for mercy. No counsel had been assigned her; she had not been questioned in her own defense; the case had been prejudged before it started; and now a child of the same parents that brought her into the world announced voluntarily that he was prepared to furnish grounds for the indictment!

Her own brother! If there had been any impression on his mind made clearer than another since his arrival on the planet, it had been that the mutual love and fraternal sympathy and helpfulness of those extraordinary people. And yet now, at the first practical test, he saw the man who had been suckled at the same breast with Zarga turn against her. His instincts revolted at the spectacle. Was Argon seizing this opportunity to pay off some secret grudge upon his sister? But surely, in that case, the court would have intervened to prevent such an outrage on even justice. So far from that, the eleven judges and Lamara herself bore every appearance of accepting the situation as a matter of course. Nor did any wave of indignation ripple through the audience. Oh, New York, with all its sins and its corruptions, would not have tolerated this! The ties of blood were sacred. But here, one might think, they granted license to attack and destroy.

Amid the mental and moral chaos into which the situation had plunged Jack, one purpose stood out clear: at the first opportunity available, at whatever risk of offending the court and defying the customs of their law, he would insist upon the demand that he himself, the party supposedly injured, should be given the right to defend this forlorn and abandoned victim. It was a right, if he chose to take it, incontestable even here. And he was ready to go to the limits of strict truth, and even a step beyond if necessary, in order to alleviate her plight. Chivalry enjoined it, and he would not be found wanting!

Meanwhile, Argon was beginning his arraignment; and it occurred to Jack that when the time came for witnesses to be called, the opportunity he awaited would arrive. He must indubitably be a witness; in fact, what other witness than himself could there be? Jim, possibly, but Jim had vanished; and though Jack would always have a warm feeling in his heart for the faithful little imp, he would sooner never set eyes on him than hear him bear hostile testimony in this matter. For the time being, he bent his attention closely on what Argon was saying.

"I thank our highest and this court," were his opening words, "for their permission to prove, before the people of Saturn, my faithful and tender love for my poor sister. Love between a brother and a sister there must always be; but the tie between Zarga and myself may perhaps be closer than common, because, as Aunion has told you, we are, though not ourselves alien among you, yet of alien linage, and thereby doubly united. You had received and trusted us as of your own community; and the joyful obligation lay upon us so to live and act among you as to justify your hospitality, and to prove that even the unruly blood of the Torides can be subdued to harmony with yours."

"Is this hypocrisy?" muttered Jack. "Can any one be deceived by it?"

He turned to fix his eyes upon Zarga. She sat there, drooping, like a lovely flower torn from its stalk; the glow and brilliance of the beauty that had been so vivid in the hall of crystal had faded as if beaten upon by storms, but she was only the more appealing to him for that reason. She did not return his look; she seemed unconscious of his presence, though she must have known he was there; but she was gazing at Argon with an expression of affection which seemed to Jack incomprehensible in the circumstances. There must be in her nature a sweetness and nobility far greater than he had hitherto imagined if she could not only forgive the attack her brother was about to make, but appear to be grateful for it!

"It is no palliation of her offense," Argon went on, "that he whom she sought to beguile was a stranger newly arrived among us; rather should that have been for her a precious opportunity to show a kindness and forbearance beyond the strict obligations of fellowship. Moreover, as you all know, and as she knew, he was already betrothed to another woman who had arrived here but a short while before him. But she was not restrained by these circumstances. She was only the more stimulated by them to pursue her course. And now I must reveal certain grievous facts which to many of you have been unsuspected."

His voice became husky, and he paused to recover himself. Zarga's face was pale and expressionless; she trembled uncontrollably, as if under a freezing wind.

"During a part of the last circuit," the speaker resumed, "she had been a pupil with me in a study of the earth from which these two strangers came. By chance, she was attracted to a youth there"—he indicated Jack—"and, through the medium of the planetary mirror used in our school, was able to follow his career closely. At first she often spoke to me of him, but latterly had seemed indifferent, her apparent change dating from the time when Miriam, our other guest, unexpectedly reached us. In truth, she had divined, by means available to initiates, that the youth was to follow, so enabling her to meet him personally; and this discovery caused what had till then been a merely fanciful and imaginative interest to kindle to a wayward and unruly passion. In spite of her knowledge of another's prior claim, she resolved, in the secrecy of her heart, to take him for herself!"

A low murmur passed through the assembly. Argon's face became stern as he manned himself for the sequel.

"My sister's relations with our highest, who loved and trusted her, gave her facilities for carrying out her project. I need not enlarge on these; but she also accepted aid from a source not only unlawful, but treasonable. She entered into a conspiracy with our hostile neighbor, the Prince of Tor, to render mutual services. He, by methods of his own, had somewhat familiarized himself with the planet of our guests, and had resolved to attempt the capture of Miriam. Zarga gave him information and aid which enabled him to succeed—after several failures—in his effort, and thus removed from her path the rival whom she feared. She was left free to practise upon the youth she pursued arts both native and magical, and by false illusions sought to persuade him that she whom he loved had betrayed him. Fortunately for all—even for her—his resistance proved invincible. Guided by intimations received from a wise friend who has long since held communication with us, we overcame the magical obstacles put in our way, and found her in the crisis of her iniquity."

The audience had listened to this narration with an interest manifestly intense. Argon, perhaps, had more to say; but he cast an imploring look at Lamara, who replied with an acquiescing and compassionate gesture which permitted him to sink back, overwrought, in his chair. Jack restrained himself for the present, perceiving that Lamara was about to speak. Would she justify Argon's cruel exposure?

Her eyes traveled over the audience, and at length rested with tenderness upon Zarga. Then she seemed, for a few moments to commune with herself.

"Evil is a false friend," she said. "Man is born asleep, and dreams in his sleep that evil is good. Only when he wakes does he recognize evil as his enemy. He begins to live when he learns that he and evil are twain. Then those twain join battle, and until the last day the issue is in doubt. The power of the enemy lies in this—that he never ceases to wear the guise of the dearest and most intimate companion, to oppose whom is to destroy life itself. And in order to win the struggle, man must plunge his sword into his inmost heart. Nothing less than that can set his true self free.

"Knowing how desperate is our own battle, we sympathize with the battle of a fellow creature. We help him by reminding him of the lie that wears the mask of truth, the hate that smiles like love, the death that calls itself life. We warn him of the treachery that stabs while it kisses. To him, in the confusion of the conflict, our succor seems like cruelty, and the draft of life to which we invite him like poison. But we are in the way of our duty, and must not falter. Until he surrenders all he held dear, his enemy is not defeated. Then the spirit enters in, and he is at peace.

"Beware of calling him who does evil, criminal! Not he, but the enemy, commits the crime. Do not condemn—defend him! Strengthen the armor of his weakness; put true weapons in his feeble hands. Love all men, but him most who most needs love. Has he harmed you? It was not he! Harm not yourself by disowning brotherhood with him!

"The sinner is poor; give him of your abundance. He has lost his way;

light your lamp to guide him. He is in prison; make him welcome in your house. He has robbed you of your treasure; give him the greater treasure of your forgiveness. He will find himself at last, and so reward you with the greatest treasure of all!

"Here, now, is our sister sorely beset," she went on, extending both her hands toward Zarga, with the light of love in her eyes. "We have suffered shame through her deed; but is not our heedlessness more in fault than she? She dwelt close to our heart, yet we failed to perceive her need. She lacked strength, yet we opened the gates of danger to her. We relaxed her with ease when she should have been strung to effort. She fell into the snare that our blindness helped to spread for her. We ask her forgiveness.

"Little sister," she continued, now addressing Zarga directly, "you are fortunate in this, that the false good you aimed at is lost to you—could never have been yours. But that is the least of your losses, and you alone, trusting to the spirit, can retrieve the rest. Take counsel with your own soul how to set about the work. All the power of our realm, which these who now look upon you represent, is yours to call upon; but a greater power stands ready to your aid, if you find humility and wisdom to accept it. Go forth with hope and courage, and be glad that all know your burden and will rejoice in your success."

In the silence that followed, Zarga went with unsteady steps to the altar and fell upon her knees there, laying hold upon it with her hands. The sun had now touched the highest point of its course, and its light fell directly upon the crystal heart. It was a spiritual test observed among Saturnians by immemorial tradition, and accounted holy. All watched breathlessly for the outcome—Argon so shaken with emotion that he could barely support himself in his seat; Jack, awe-stricken and wondering.

After a moment the crystal slowly brightened; soon it had become so bright that the eye could hardly endure the dazzle of it. A sparkling vapor arose from it; living tongues of pure flame flickered up and increased; the stone was now a blaze of fire. At last none save Lamara could sustain the luster of it. The vast assemblage lifted up its voice in a majestic sound of recognition and acceptance of the judgment. As the flame vanished, the spectators assumed their veils, and the enormous auditorium appeared empty. The high court was dissolved. Zarga was no longer to be seen.

Lamara descended from her throne, and was joined by Aunion. She beckoned to Jack and Argon, and the four passed out of the amphitheater together.

CHAPTER XXVI
THE ELIXIR

JACK was so much dazed by what he had seen and heard that he could find nothing to say to Lamara, or to Aunion either. The slope from the amphitheater led down to the beach, where a boat was in waiting. Lamara, who had been conversing apart with Aunion, now addressed Jack.

"I must leave you in Argon's care. We shall soon meet again. We, no more than you, know what is to come. We cannot promise that what you wish will come to pass; but we sometimes live to be thankful for hopes unfulfilled. The spirit always gives us what we need. You have friends; have patience!"

The ominous purport which Jack was prone to put upon her words was somewhat counteracted by the smile which accompanied the touch of her finger-tips in farewell. She and her minister boarded the craft, and Jack and Argon were alone.

"I don't know that I shall ever be wise enough to comprehend all this," Jack remarked; "but I shall never be quite the same fool that I was before. I feel, without knowing why, that what seemed cruel in your speech was love and mercy. As for Lamara, she lives and speaks in a world and a language beyond me. And yet I believe that something in me deeper than my mind understands her. Perhaps I've never known myself, and that is why I know nothing."

"The best generally comes last," said Argon. "I've lived twenty times as long as you, but what small light I have comes from others, and with difficulty. What I said to-day was born of the thinking of men wiser and better than I shall ever be. What I wanted was to take that poor child in my arms and comfort her. But, thanks to the spirit, and to Lamara, and to the societies, I was able to rise to a higher love of her than that!"

"What will Zarga do?" Jack inquired.

"I think the shock she got from that sapphire charm of yours began a vital alteration in her, which events happening afterward confirmed and gave direction to," said his friend. "She had been in a morbid state. I doubt if she really cared for you—in that way—at all. Your adventure in coming here stirred her imagination, and the impulse of rivalry with Miriam roused her vanity and ambition. Then, no doubt, Torpeon led her on. Probably, too, some indiscretions on your part and Miriam's helped the conspirators. But nothing irrevocable, so far as I know, has happened yet."

Having none of the vanity of amorous conquest, Jack was relieved to learn that Zarga's infatuation might be unsubstantial. But he returned to his question.

"No one can foretell her plans," was Argon's answer. "But I'm sure she'll never be content with anything less than trying her utmost to undo the mischief she has done. And in spite of her light manner, she really is a girl of remarkable qualities. Lamara, as you heard, gives her her full confidence and unrestricted liberty. I dare say she is at work already. For that matter, there's no time to lose; and we must realize that the situation is serious. Torpeon will go all lengths!"

"I hope I needn't tell you that I had sense enough to understand from what Lamara said to-day, that forgiveness of the enemy is not only your belief, but your practise. That implies that I ought to forgive Torpeon. But if evil be our only enemy, then it is his as well as mine; and if I can take a hand in preventing the evil he intends, I shall be doing him a friendly service. Of course, it won't be easy to bear in mind the distinction between his evil and himself; but I'll promise to try my best! I won't try to kill him; I'll go no further than to use every means possible to get Miriam away from him; and then, if he puts his evil away, I'll forgive him with all my heart! It seems to me Lamara herself shouldn't ask more! And I don't see that I can ask less."

The candor of this plea tempted Argon to smile; but he put a hand affectionately on Jack's shoulder and replied: "I agree with you!"

"That's a comfort!" rejoined the other. "Now, as it seems plain I can do nothing here, can't you give me a lift over to Tor?

"That is not for me to decide," Argon answered. "I know only in part the present state of things; but I know that several forces are working together in behalf of Miriam and you. They are powerful forces; humanly speaking, they could hardly be more so. On the other hand, Torpeon is putting forth his whole strength, which is very formidable, and no scruples will restrain him. But neither you nor I know the plan of campaign on either side; so that if we were to break in on our own account, we might happen to do more harm than good. Just as a parallel example, suppose Miriam had carried out that experiment a while ago!"

Jack reddened. "A woman in extremity has a right to the protection of death."

"That lies between her and the spirit," said Argon.

"May not the spirit work through me?"

Argon was silent.

"I don't know what other plans there may be," Jack resumed. "My plan is to be with her, to save her if I can; if not, to die with her. Who else is so much concerned as I?"

He was speaking with the utmost energy, but with self-control. Argon was conscious of an increase of moral stature in him; he felt the contagion of his mood and the justice of his argument. But yonder swung the red planet, beyond the reach of either of them. The young Saturnian had no power at his personal disposal to bridge the distance. Such adventures could be undertaken only by cooperation of larger means. He recalled Lamara's words at parting, "The spirit gives us what we need!" With all his heart, at that moment, he shared his friend's longing for light and aid.

They were standing but a few rods from the entrance of the amphitheater. Argon, whose eyes were turned in that direction, saw some one emerge from the portal who did not at once move toward them, or seem to be aware of their propinquity. He appeared to be contemplating the great structure, and thoughtfully estimating its architectural qualities and proportions. He rested a hand upon one of the huge pillars of the entrance, and examined a design wrought upon it by the unknown artist who had taken part in the erection of the only building in Saturn which was permanent. Argon himself had often studied this design, executed in low relief and representing a flowering rose-bush growing out of a skull. The stranger traced the outlines with his finger. Argon had never fathomed the meaning of the symbol, which belonged to an era removed immeasurably from the present. Who could this stranger be who interested himself in Saturnian problems of archeology? He was not a Saturnian; his dress was unfamiliar, and he bore the insignia of none of the great societies.

The man now turned his face seaward, and perceived the others. He made a courteous gesture of salutation, but remained where he was. Jack, who now observed him for the first time, was seize with an unaccountable curiosity or interest. The aspect of the unknown was so cordial and inviting that the two youths were insensibly drawn toward him.

He was of commanding stature, with a light and lofty carriage of head and shoulders, and a grace of posture and movement which indicated the vigor of manhood in its prime. He wore an undergarment of a lustrous tissue woven of gold and white threads, reaching half-way down his thigh, and a short, white cloak with a deep-violet hem. Sandals were on his feet; his head was uncovered, except by the wavy curls of his yellow hair. The smile in his eyes stirred also the corners of his lips, and his whole countenance conveyed an impression of good fellowship, intelligence, and effectiveness such as made impossibilities seem easy and discouragement absurd. Life, in his companionship, would be uninterrupted achievement and delight; and this was so obvious at the first glance that he immediately wore the guise of a tried and familiar friend, though neither Jack nor Argon could recall having ever before seen him.

"You have an admirable building here," he remarked, "and I'm glad to see it is still in use. It belongs to a date when the earth and man used to work together in a way rather different from now. You have made improvements since then, and yet some interesting secrets have been forgotten. This carving now—can either of you young men explain its use and significance?"

He looked from one to another with an expression so bright and pregnant as to have the effect of an overflowing fountain of wisdom, ready to irrigate and render fruitful all the world's deserts of ignorance. Jack offered no reply, though he was possessed by the conviction that he and this wonderful stranger could not have met for no purpose, so profoundly intimate and kindly was his regard, and so great withal was his moral and intellectual ascendancy. He was a king of men, but democratic and simple as a boon comrade.

"I have puzzled over it many times," Argon answered; "but neither I nor our wise ones could solve it. The secret was lost, as you say, many thousands of lives ago."

"Nothing truly done or thought is ever lost, however," rejoined the stranger. "The secret waits in its place till the need for it returns. As for this particular enigma, I happened to know the sculptor who wrought it well; and he and I helped each other in turn to place this section of the shaft. Apparently it's never been opened since!"

"You!" exclaimed Argon in a reverential tone. "You are an immortal, then!"

The other glanced up with a laugh. "Why, so are we all! But I'm one of the travelers. When I was a little fellow I used to stare up in the sky at night, and tell myself that some time I'd visit those bright places up there and make friends with the folks that lived in them. Well, there are a good many of them, and I'm still in the early stages of my journey; but there are persons worth knowing in all of them, and my circle of friends is enlarging! One of these days, if you like," he added, turning to Jack, "I'll take you about a little and introduce you. But as to this design: it stands, of course, for a word in the universal language, but you would probably be more interested in seeing the thing that it covers. Let's try if these old joints and hinges are still in working order."

The pillar was a massive monolith, of a diameter twice the height of a man. He laid hold of it, seizing it in both arms, and put forth his strength to drag it toward the left. The broad muscles of his chest and arms rounded out under the skin, but for a moment the column did not yield. Jack was about to offer his aid, though the enterprise seemed utterly impossible; but just then the great shaft started, and slid smoothly and noiselessly on its base, disclosing an aperture in the plinth below. The whole column had been swung aside.

The stranger stepped back, turning a pleased smile upon the onlookers, like a boy successful in a feat of strength or skill.

"We were pretty fair workmen in those days," he observed; "our rule and square were true! Now, what do you say—shall we have a look inside?"

Jack started forward, his heart on fire with anticipation of some good event, he knew not what. Argon followed. In the cavity of the plinth there was the shining of a box finely wrought in gold; it was covered with work in high relief, but of what design could not be discerned in the obscurity of the receptacle. The stranger grasped the box by the corners and lifted it out into the clear daylight.

It was foursquare, about a cubit in height, and half as much on the side. The lid was pyramidal, with a winged figure on the apex. The entire surface of the object was carved over with a representation of a clambering rose-vine, amid the interstices of which were numerous little golden skeletons, some of them caught in the snare, other forcing their way actively between the branches. There was enough conventionalism in the treatment to preserve its dignity. The effect was grotesque, but grave.

The stranger now turned back the lid on its hinge, revealing a tall beaker, with panels of clear crystal set in gold and enriched with precious stones. He took it out of the box and set it down on a corner of the plinth. It bore a cover, and was half filled with some transparent liquid which sparkled like melted diamonds.

"There is a draft which few living men would venture to swallow," the stranger remarked with an enigmatic smile. "The recipe for its making has been sought by many since then, but was never recovered. It is said to possess the property of enabling the drinker to win the desire of his heart; but if there be any doubt or falsehood in him, it will destroy him forever. Would you care to taste of it?"

His eyes were upon Jack as he spoke. There was a challenge in them, and yet warning. As Jack met the look, he knew who the stranger was. Solarion was come to offer him all he loved and longed for in life, but at the risk, should he prove unworthy, of death. It was the choice which, in some form, is submitted to every human creature at some epoch in his career. Jack laid a hand on the handle of the beaker, but paused.

"There's no doubt in me of my love for her," he said, addressing this mysterious messenger with a certain stateliness of manner not customary with him, but befitting the solemnity of the occasion. "But I'm a man, and no angel. There are things I've thought and done which I wish had been otherwise. Tell me this: if I fail, what will become of her?"

"I cannot answer," replied Solarion. "But God deals with us all alike."

Jack turned the words over in his mind. "I'm content!" he said at length.

He uncovered the beaker, from which rose immediately a marvelous fragrance that dispensed itself in the air about them. He had a glimpse of the troubled face of Argon, and exchanged a mute farewell with him.

The last thing he saw was Solarion, who stood in a meditative posture, one hand resting on the golden box, and his eyes fixed unswervingly upon him. Then, with the image of Miriam filling his soul, he raised the cup to his lips and drank.

CHAPTER XXVII
DISASTER

TORPEON, after receiving the signal that Miriam wished to speak with him, was on his way down the main staircase of the castle when he met a servant hurrying in the opposite direction. The man, at the sight of him, stopped and made his obeisance. He was panting and evidently frightened.

"Well," said Torpeon, with a note of stern interrogation.

"Gracious prince," faltered the man, "it has fallen into the river!"

Torpeon was silent for a moment, frowning upon the messenger. "What is this?"

"No. 19, Supreme One! The bank fell in and the laboratory went with it!"

It may be observed that the castle stood on a high point of ground on the broad delta between the two largest rivers that emptied into the Bitter Sea. On streets radiating from it were the houses of the capital city of Tor; they were of uniform design and moderate size; each enclosed a central court, in which the inhabitants spent their days and pursued their occupations; the rooms were used for sleeping only. All the dwellings were connected by a system of vibratory transmitters, centering in a receiving-station in the basement of the castle, enabling Torpeon to issue orders to any household or to obtain information of its activities when he pleased. Beyond the circumference of the city proper, which was of no great area, were the laboratories, twenty-seven in number, constructed along the banks of the two rivers, and isolated from the approach of any person not employed in them. They were carefully guarded, and the nature of the industries carried on in them was never allowed to transpire. The precautions taken made any intrusion upon the workers, or interference with their operations, practically impossible. So, at least, Torpeon had believed.

Of these laboratories No. 19 was at this time engaged in an important part of the complicated scheme which Torpeon was prosecuting. Outwardly, it had the aspect of a dome, or hemisphere, of steel, with foundations in the solid rock. Such strength was required, not so much for protection against attack from without, as to secure it against disturbance from the experiments carried on within. Some of these would have shaken to pieces any building of ordinary design and materials.

"You know the penalty for false reports?" said Torpeon quietly.

The man's teeth chattered. The form of torture referred to was searching enough to deter the most reckless liar. But he stuck to his story.

"It is truth, Mightiness," he quavered. "The rock was undermined, and—"

"Come with me," Torpeon interrupted. "Speak to no one. If you are confirmed, I will promote you; if not—" He made a gesture sufficiently explanatory.

He led the way back to his private chamber, postponing for the time his conference with Miriam. A glance at the pentagonal plate as he entered the room was enough to show him that the report had been no flight of imagination. He seated himself at the table and concentrated all his faculties upon the situation.

The indicator for No. 19 was wavering loosely back and forth, and responded to no efforts to extract information. He tested No. 20. After a short interval the sign of attention was received. "Has anything unusual occurred?" he asked, in a tone which he divested of any emotion.

Rapidly and confusedly the message was poured into his ear from the annunciator:

"Assistant on the way with full details. The collapse was sudden and complete. No. 19; also a shock in No. 7 and instruments displaced. Does not appear to be seismic. Sheer cleavage of rock between us and No. 19. Building overset in bed of river. Operators drowned. No explosive sounds. Guards report no one seen in neighborhood. Selections of stations indicates design. Circuit interrupted. Fear further disturbances. No. 5—" There was a break, and then, faintly and agitatedly, "Your presence seems urgent."

Torpeon rose from the table. He moved a lever, which disconnected the plate and closed the annunciator. His bearing was composed, and he smiled nonchalantly upon the trembling servant who had been standing beside the doorway.

"You were partly correct," he said adjusting his mantle and taking up a short truncheon from a shelf beside the table. He detached from it a metal ring, stamped with the device of a triangle within a square. "Take this to the captain of the guard—it is your warrant of authority—and tell him to hold a hundred men in readiness. The matter is of slight importance, but we may have to enforce a little discipline. After delivering the order, return here, and keep watch outside this door till I come back. If any one attempts to enter, put him under arrest. If he resists, kill him. Give no information and answer no questions. Have you understood me?"

"Yes, gracious prince!"

Motioning the man to precede him, he closed the door behind them; the messenger hurried away on his errand, and Torpeon departed with a leisurely step down the corridor.

Never before, however, had the Prince of Tor felt such consternation as now. He was being attacked by an enemy who seemed to be cognizant of his plans, and who was able to overcome his precautions and produce inexplicable results. He could not doubt that Lamara must be the unseen power behind the attack, and that she meant to defeat his great enterprise. How she had divined his purpose he could only conjecture; and he was amazed that she had so far departed from traditional Saturnian custom as to undertake offensive operations. He had not counted upon such an innovation, and could not estimate her resources. That they might prove superior to his own seemed not improbable. She had already annulled the painfully devised measures by which he had believed his undertaking could be secretly carried out, and he be beyond reach of pursuit or hindrance before it was discovered.

Nevertheless he would not admit failure. If he were prevented from prosecuting his first plan, there was yet a desperate alternative left. Nor would he surrender Miriam. If the end of all things earthly were to come for him, she would perish with him. And perhaps, with her as a hostage, he might be able to parley with the enemy, and obtain terms which his unaided power was inadequate to secure. But, at best, the outlook was dark.

He left the castle by a private way, and was conveyed by an instantaneous subterranean route to the scene of the disaster to the laboratories. The spectacle was even more sinister than he anticipated.

The volume of water rushing down the river-bed was much greater than ever before, dark in color, and sweeping with it huge masses of drift and wreckage. Whirlpools had been formed at various points, which sucked in and again tossed aloft fragments of buildings and bodies of animals, some human ones among them. The ruins of No. 19 formed a sort of island in the midst of the headlong stream, against which it raged like a snarling wild beast, gnawing at it with its foaming fangs, and ever and anon tearing shreds of it away. The rocky headland on which No. 20 stood had been partly undermined, and the structure was held at a slant, threatening momentarily to subside altogether. Nos. 7 and 5 were out of sight round a bend of the river, but there was no reason to suppose that their plight was better than the others. The long-sought results of Toridian science were brought to naught.

The wild-looking figure of a man appeared round the headland of No. 20, and came running in Torpeon's direction, tossing up his arms and shouting insanely. He was half naked, bony and hairy, and swung a sling in his hand. On catching sight of Torpeon he halted, and at first turned to flee; but, taking courage, faced about again, and snatching a sharp-cornered stone from his girdle sent it whizzing at the prince from his sling. Torpeon raised the truncheon that he carried, and the stone was deflected from its course and fell harmlessly. The man started to escape, but the truncheon, pointed at him, took the power from his legs, and he fell to the ground.

Torpeon went up to him as he lay groveling, and turned him over with his foot.

"So this is my friend, Krotox!" he said with a low chuckle. "It's a pleasure to meet with you again so soon!"

"Sublime prince, spare me!" whimpered the creature. "I have done nothing. I will reveal all I know!"

"I should be sorry to give you that trouble," Torpeon replied. "But I am looking for reports from No. 19; I will send you to hasten them."

He took up the wriggling wretch by a leg and arm and carried him to the brink of the torrent. Krotox shrieked and chattered like a hyena. The prince swung him to and fro and far out into the turmoil of waters. The current snatched him, and in a moment dashed his head against an abutment of the steel dome. Torpeon watched the dead body drift downward, revolve in an eddy, and pass out of sight.

"Can it be Lamara who uses such instruments?" he muttered. "If this be a mere insurrection of the exiles, there is more hope than I feared."

He turned and strode away toward No. 20.

CHAPTER XXVIII
BATTLE

JIM ducked his head in a delighted greeting to Miriam and performed a wave of salutation with his crutch. "Dey can't lose us, miss," he remarked.

Miriam regarded him with increasing pleasure and cordiality. Here was a creature, absolutely trustworthy and highly intelligent, come to her at a moment when she was most in need of precisely such a person. "Did you come alone?" was her instinctive question.

"Don't let dat worry yer, miss," was his reply. "I's John de Baptis', hollerin' in der wilderness; de rest of de bunch mebbe don' know where deir goin', but dey's on de way! We's goin' to clean up dis here back yard, an' den we'll prepare de chamber for de bridegroom! As fer honeymoon, how'd N'York suit yer? Dere's more moons 'n honey round dese diggin's!"

"But what news of Jack? Any message? Is he well?"

"Say, miss; wait till yer lamps him! De boss is fine—he's out er sight! 'Bout de las' I seen uv him he was feedin' his face wid de best roast p'easant 'tween dis an' Delmonniker's, an' washin' her down wid de right juice, believe me! Sure, he'd a message all fixed up fer yer, pink goods, an' smellin' like a Fif' Av'noo drug-joint; but me, I meets up on a suddint wid dat dere shiny gink—you knows him, de front name uv him is Sol—an' he stakes me for de trip dat quick I didn't git no time fer ter grab de billydux. Mebbe yer'll have it by der reg'lar post!"

Having thus avouched his fitness for diplomatic interludes, Jim cast an approving look around him, and congratulated the lady on the homelike aspect of her surroundings. "Dis here come-an'-go stuff gits my goat," he observed with feeling, "I dassent go fer to sit on a chair fer fear some guy 'll t'ink it away from me! An' de scenery dey rings in on yer—say, don' it swat yer between de peepers? De sky gits too busy wid itself, what wid moons an' rings an' truck like dat! No, miss, Broadway was never like dis! An' de gals—well, not presumin' ter speak uv yerself, miss, dat Jenny ain't no half-tone—she's de stuff!"

After reassuring her visitor as to the stability of her chairs, Miriam seated herself opposite to him, and begged him to disclose his plans.

"Fust off, I'll put yer wise to meself," he began, dropping his voice to a confidential undertone. "Dis here Sol geezer, he's a dead-game sport an' no come-back; he sizes up what I's goin' ag'inst, an' he dolls me up wid a new suit o' interplex, an' manipperlates me ol' hobble-stick inter a Paggysis an' de Empire State Limited, an' I dunno what nex'; but when I needs it, I has it! Wid dis stick in me han', ol' Torpy's got nuttin' on us, miss, an' I gives yer dat straight!"

Miriam had already noticed signs of peculiar animation in the crutch, and she lent an interested ear to what was to follow.

"Lissen here, miss," Jim continued, hitching his chair nearer. "Torpy, he ain't no back-number, at dat; an' he fixes up a play dat would beat us sure, on'y fer de Sol outfit an' anudder t'ing or two. I's been romancin' roun' dis ranch, quiet like, as me nater is, an' I'm onter his curves. Dere's just one trouble wid you, miss, speakin' as frien's, you's too much of a good-looker, an' you sure gits Torpy dat nutty on yer he'd bust up de hull universe sooner'n lose yer; an' me, I ain't sayin' yer ain't wort' it!"

"Jim, your compliments are wonderful," said Miriam; "but please—"

"In course, miss. It's like dis—Torpy's figgerin' to slip de hawser o' dis here dinky lil moon o' his, an' go cavortin' roun' de solar system, unhitchin' all de odder eart's as he sails by, an' fetchin' up at de sun. He changes cars dere—de sun 'd be some too hot fer my tastes, but likely he takes a cooler along—an heads de process'un fer O'Brien's belt an' de milky way! A sort o' Cook's tour, puss-nel conducted, see? An' you along, eatin' ice cream an' chattin' sociable like: 'Gimme a new batch o' stars ter-morrer, Torpy,' you says; 'dis lot is some tarnished, an' outer fashion, anyway,' you tells him. 'Right-o!' he comes back. Down goes de clutch, an' ho, fer de boun'-less main! Dat's Torpy!"

Miriam shook her head and smiled sadly. "I've seen something of what magic and do, Jim," she said; "but I think you have been deceived. After all, there is such a thing as reality!"

"Magic, nuttin'!" retorted Jim; "dis here game is sci'ntific! Torpy's been coachin' up on de gravitation stunt; he's had his sci'nce sharps workin' overtime dese five years on de job to fix up a counter to it; an' dey gets de hull t'ing ready ter touch off at sunup ter-morrer! Ain't I been t'rough de lab'ratories an' seen 'em at it!"

"If such a thing were possible," began Miriam. But she reflected that the discussion was unprofitable, whether or not the possibility existed. "What we must think of," she said, "is whether anything can be done to escape. I have a plan of my own, but only for the last resort." She hesitated, but resolved to trust the gnome with her secret. "In that room," she went on, "is an instrument for atomic disintegration, which I have adjusted so that by merely reversing the magnetic field, Tor would be exploded into dust. I tell you this, Jim, because should there be no other hope, and I be unable to reach the machine myself, I should ask you to act in my place!"

Jim eyed her admiringly. "Say, miss, speakin' o' game sports, you's a top-liner! Le's take a slant at de outfit." She led the way to the laboratory, and found no difficulty in explaining the mechanism of the machine, Jim, as has been noted, having a natural aptitude for all mechanical contrivances. He handled the magnet with a touch suggestive of the innate longing of the unregenerate small boy to unleash the elements of destruction. But he virtuously mastered the inclination. "She's a sure-enough peach, miss," he said, stepping back with a sigh; "but we's ain't needin' her. An' anudder t'ing, Torpy's a slob, all right; but he's up ag'in a stiff game, an' you's de stakes he's playin' fer; an' I puts it to you straight, kin yer blame him? Ef he'd got de strangle clutch on yer, it 'ud be all right to pull de gun on him, 'cause we's bound ter win, anyway; but we's got him beat, dough he don't know it yit; an' what I says is, when he does know it, dat's punishment enough fer him, an' we kin let it go at dat! Let him keep his ol' moon, an' spen' his declinin' years sorrerin' over de error uv his ways an' de loss uv all he helt mos' dear! Say, a'ter I's had me chin wid him, yer 'll see him takin' water like an ol' boozer de mornin' a'ter a wet night—d' yer git me! I's goin' ter han' him some home trut's—dat's me! An' when you an' me starts our slide fer home-base, yer 'll see Torpy a gazin' at us in a wild su'mize, like dat dago gink in Cent'al America musin' on de ruins o' Cart'age!"

In spite of the radiant self-confidence thus poetically expressed, Miriam could not help feeling a little uneasy. She had no desire to annihilate Torpeon if she might escape on any terms less tragic; but was Jim as well equipped as he imagined for the undertaking? What could he or she know of Torpeon's resources?

"You spoke of seeing his laboratories," she said. "What if the work they are doing should be accomplished before we can act? And what prevented Jack, or some of the Saturnians, from coming here with you?"

Jim had no objection to treating facts with the imaginative coloring proper to his temperament, but he recognized the prudence of discrimination in this case. Miriam must not be led to suppose that Jack had neglected her; and yet, if she learned of the complication with Zarga, she might feel some distress.

"Dis here is de age uv splittin' jobs, miss," he explained. "Me an' Sol is tendin' dis end, an' de boss an' de Sattum gang is busy fixin' up t'ings fer de getaway when we's t'rough here. De lab-ratories," he hastened on, "has got deirs befo' I seen yer. I can't tell no lies; I chops 'em down wid me lil crutchet, like de fader uv his country! I picks up a bunch o' bums here an' dere as I comes roun', an' gives 'em de tip to fire de pop'lar heart an' work a French revolution stunt on Torpy to distrac' his min'; an' by the rumpus dey's raisin'," he added, breaking off as a noise of tumult made itself audible outside the castle, "I figgers me orders is bein' obeyed!"

The door opened and Jenny, her pink cheeks streaked with pallor and her eyes round with consternation, ran into the room with a tale of terror:

"Oh, if your please, miss, the mob is broke loose and we'll all be murthered in our beds! They've fetched ladders and torches, for all the world like the history-books, and the garrison is parleying with the ringleaders, and us without our traveling-dresses! Oh, wurra-wurra! Whatever will become of us?"

Miriam was not inaccessible to imaginative fears; but anything like a menace of actual danger restored her composure. She silenced Jenny with a contemptuous gesture and walked to the window.

A disorderly crowd of strange-looking people, constantly increasing in numbers, was collecting in front of the castle. They evidently meant mischief; but Miriam recognized at once that only the treason of those who composed the defenders could involve any immediate peril. She had no reason to doubt that Torpeon was competent to impose order, in any case; and, assuming that he was still in the castle, she expected him to appear. But he was nowhere to be seen. She recalled that she had been expecting him to visit her at the moment when Jim entered. She was now aware, of course, how he had been prevented.

A shower of stones hurled by the mob smashed some windows in the lower part of the castle. The garrison made no counter-demonstration; and there were signs which might indicate that Jenny's statement about a parley was not all fancy.

Jim, at Miriam's side, was contemplating the scene with grunts and chuckles of manifest satisfaction. But he did not lose his critical acumen.

"Dese here guys don't know de ropes," he remarked. "What's brickbats an' hollerin' in a play like dis? Dinnermite's de stuff! But I figgers Torpy's cornered de supply! He'll show his han' befor' long!"

"Will I be after makin' a rope of the bedclothes to let down the back winder, miss?" suggested Jenny, still palpitating.

"Jim is the captain of the watch," Miriam replied with a smile.

"We's neutral, miss, in dis here scrimmage," Jim informed her, assuming the gravity of a commander. "De more Torpy an' dat bunch lams de life out o' each odder, de more us gives 'em de merry ha-ha! When dey gits t'rough, we deals wid de remains; we rides the whirlwin' an' direcks de storm! Dere's one o' my boys now!" he exclaimed—"dat fat duck wid his pants gone—Asgar—dat's him! He's hoopin' it up to beat de band! What's gone wrong wid Krotox? Mebbe he's fell by de wayside!"

"Oh, if Jack were here!" thought Miriam, as a fresh volley of stones crashed against the walls. "No!" she added in the same breath; "thank God he isn't!"

The next moment she faced about with a violent start and a leap of the heart. Had she heard Jack's voice speak her name, close to her ear? But no one was there!

She was about to call out his name—to shriek it out; but she silenced it on her lips. Was it not, rather, as if a hand—his hand—touched her mouth in warning? Assuredly he was here. She could not be mistaken in the sense of his neighborhood. Never, even in his more physical presence, had she been more convinced of it. And yet, save for Jim and Jenny, who were absorbed in the scene outside the window, the room was empty. What did this mean?

It was, somehow, different from the physical invisibility of the Saturnians. The influence was not like that; it was a spiritual vibration. Was Jack dead, then?

She felt, on the contrary, that he had never been more alive.

CHAPTER XXIX
PARADISE POSTPONED

SOLARION caught the crystal cup as it dropped from Jack's hand, and with his other arm supported his body as it fell. Argon uttered a cry of dismay. But meeting the other's eyes, which were now filled with a soft but almost insupportable light, he recognized the benign significance behind the apparent calamity.

"We will let the body rest in the plinth," Solarion said, lifting it as he spoke into the cavity, and replacing the cup and its golden receptacle. "He is honest and brave, all will go well with him. Tell Lamara he stood the test, and that I will meet her here on the hour appointed."

The light grew brighter and Argon, perforce, closed his eyelids. When he looked again the column of the portal occupied its former position, and he was alone.

Of these things Jack knew nothing.

The reaching out of his spirit toward Miriam, at the moment of swallowing the elixir, had dominated all other thoughts and impulses, and by operation of spiritual law, his immaterial entity, disembarrassed from the physical, at once was swept in her direction. Distances between persons, on the spiritual plane, where nothing operates to delay the inclinations of the mind, are necessarily and immediately determined by sympathies or repulsions, as the case may be, existing between them; and, as the separation from each other of the poles of the sidereal universe hardly suffices to indicate the gulf that yawns between incompatible natures and temperaments, so, between those who love each other, a handbreadth is still too far apart. Nothing else is possible in a sphere where all things live and the inertia of lifeless matter is not.

Jack, accordingly, soon became aware that he was in Miriam's vicinity; but he was at first perplexed by an unconsidered circumstance of their mutual conditions.

The physical eye is fashioned to perceive material objects only; it is powerless to discern the forms of thoughts or the color of emotions. And in the spiritual plane, emotion and thought constitute, respectively, the substance and the shape of things seen. On the other hand, the spiritual eye is not less unable to have cognizance of material things; and the two worlds are thus effectively disjoined one from the other. Of course, the spirit incarnate is none the less in constant relations with the spirit disincarnate; but both alike are insensible, normally, to that fact.

Jack, during his journey from our earth to Saturn, had already experienced disincarnation; but inasmuch as his environment had then been also spiritual, he had felt no discrepancy between it and himself. Now, however, he, a spirit, was confronted with material surroundings, and must depend on methods of communication more subtle than those of spiritual sight and touch in order to make his presence felt, or himself to establish consciousness of the medium in which he sought to operate.

How was he to bring the world in which he was into practical relations with that which she occupied, since neither could she see nor touch him, nor he, her? This seemed like to prove an awkward obstacle in the way of what he aimed to accomplish.

But must not Solarion have foreseen this difficulty? And would he have deliberately mocked him, through the agency of the elixir, with a useless gift? The idea was preposterous! There must be some way of solving the problem.

He stood motionless, like a man in the darkness of an unfamiliar place, and set himself to the task of withdrawing from his outward sphere of consciousness. He was presently rewarded by the perception of the gradual emergence of an inner consciousness; it was as if the pupils of the eyes of the man in the dark place, slowly expanding, were becoming sensitive to rays of light before unperceived.

A path of communication between the two worlds did, then, exist. It was not normally accessible, because its existence was unsuspected; but when intelligently sought, it might be found. And Jack realized that if it were accessible to him, from his side, it must also be accessible to Miriam from hers. The inner consciousness, in her and in him, was a sort of common ground between them, in which they could meet and have intercourse. It was neither spiritual wholly, nor wholly material, but an intermediate region. Nor was there anything radically strange in this; had he not, in the earthly life, often felt aware of her proximity before his corporeal senses informed him of it, and had he been blindfolded, would not the touch of her hand have exerted an influence distinguishable from the touch of any other? If he were alive to such intuitions, much more should she, with her finer organization, be so.

Greatly encouraged by his discovery, Jack proceeded to put it to the trial.

Without having intelligently traced his course, he had been brought to the suite of rooms which Miriam occupied. They appeared to him in shadowy form, much like the reflection of objects seen in a plate of glass, and not so distant as in a mirror. But as he grew more accustomed to the situation, the distinctness increased.

He was at first puzzled by the similarity of the rooms to those seen on his own earth; and he wondered for a moment whether Miriam could have returned to their planet during the interval of their separation. But a more concentrated scrutiny soon revealed the magical character of the appearance. Whether the magic were black or white he did not pause to determine. Here, at all events, was a laboratory, and he recognized it as the one which he had already seen in Lamara's water-mirror. It was perhaps because of the intense emotional stress which Miriam had undergone here that he had been first led to it. But she was not here now. He glanced at the apparatus on the table and comprehended the method of its operation. He could even discern the electrons in the atom in their revolution around one another, and form an estimate of the stupendous force which would be liberated by their dissociation. But matters more urgent claimed his attention.

He passed through the doorway into the adjoining chamber; the door had been left ajar, and he was careful to go through the opening, which was somewhat narrow for his bulk, and to keep his feet to the level of the floor. He felt that he could not push the door farther open, and he did not know that he could have passed through the substance of it; it seemed to him proper to observe, so far as possible, the natural limitations amid which he found himself. It aided his recognition of them.

Upon entering the chamber he saw Miriam, with two others, standing near the window. He paid no heed to the others, nor did he see them with nearly the distinctness with which the woman he loved appeared to him. Was it her, or her spirit, that he saw? At moments it seemed to be the one, then the other. From one standpoint, indeed, they were identical. Yet there was a difference; but it was she!

A powerful irradiation of joy streamed forth from him. It was both visible and invisible to Jack himself. As a spiritual emanation, it welled out toward her and enveloped her, so that he fancied she must be aware of it—the roseate glory of it, shot through with golden quiverings. Then, remembering that the natural eye could not discern it, he was surprised to see her move slightly, as if some faint sound or remembered scent had caught her attention. But in a moment she again turned her gaze out of the window.

He approached the group. What—Jim! Undoubtedly it was Jim, but something in the presentation perplexed him—two quite distinguishable Jims, though the same; but one was the grotesque little urchin he knew, the other—he had known nothing of this wonderful brightness, as if the boy were full of light; and surely there were two complete and well-formed legs! That crutch, too; was it a crutch—or was it—what was it? Jim was speaking; it was the familiar street-gamin lingo; but within it, or above it, was another language, which Jack understood with his spiritual hearing, which conveyed beautiful things—affection, loyalty, courage, resource—qualities which the terrestrial Jim would stare even to hear mentioned. Yet they belonged to him as much as did his own patter—far more so, indeed.

The young woman who made the third of the group was manifested but dimly, for Jack had never made Jenny's acquaintance, and perceived no more than an agreeable something of feminine purport. In truth, it had been with the side-glance only of his mind that he had observed these persons; it was Miriam who filled and overflowed the central scope of his vision. How beautiful and adorable she was! He had loved and adored her previously to the poor extent of his mortal compass; but now he saw loveliness and splendor—an harmonious interfusing of soul and flesh—an illumination of the transient with the deathless—such as made him blush with a kind of divine embarrassment, as if he had no right to such a revelation. Was it possible that a creature so transcendent loved him?

"Miriam, Miriam!" he muttered.

Ah! She had heard him! What a start she gave; and as she turned, the marvelous glory of her aura flashed out and mingled with him. He felt the beating of her heart as if it were his own, and her nerves thrilling in rime with his. She was about to utter his name, but something prompted him to make a gesture of silence. This was not the moment to make known their secret. Gazing at her, he saw the misgiving of his death shudder through her, and spontaneously there surged from him a response so tumultuous with inexhaustible life that she was at once reassured. She did not yet understand, but she knew!

He had learned much concerning his own state and powers in the few moments of his sojourn here, but Miriam's initiation was almost instantaneous. Love opened all gates and shone through all windows; and her incarnate self took him by the hand and gave him full consciousness on the earthly plane, while retaining his spiritual powers. She, on her side, combined with her natural senses the perception of what was above the natural, and saw him and what belonged to his state as he saw her and hers. Such a fulness of communion was ineffable. Their auras blended and kindled into new exaltations, brimming with speech and vision. The pages of their memories lay open before them as living pictures of the events recorded, to be comprehended at a glance; and words spoken in the spirit conveyed significances which no eloquent volubility of earthly tongues could rival. Nevertheless, this boundless speech, descending from its superior degree into the lower, took on there the outward form of mortal utterances, as the endlessness of productivity is enclosed in the simple seed sown in the soil. Conversing together in what, to earthly ears, would seem the simplest terms, they could impart to each other kingdoms of meanings intelligible to the imperial soul.

He and Miriam now stood side by side at the window, and he found himself able to look freely through her material eyes. The swaying and struggling of the mob and its confused uproar were visible and audible to him. A sorry spectacle! But though immeasurably remote from him, and unimportant, he realized that Miriam was still in the toils of it. And he had come hither to rescue her!

Her thought spoke to him. "Dearest, will you not take me where you are? You are free from earth; why may not I be so, also?"

The death of the body, the deliverance of the spirit, and immortality of love unhindered for them! A touch on the instrument in the next room could compass it!"

"La, miss, it's gone that hot, all of a sudden!" remarked Jenny, pushing back the hair from her moist forehead; "like them July days on the beach last summer! Whatever ails me I don't know!" She was enveloped in the fervent sphere of the lovers' hearts.

"Dere he comes! Pipe ol' Torpy over dere!" cried Jim, pointing excitedly to the outskirts of the crowd. "Good t'ing de boss ain't here; he'd be runnin' out and git his nut busted! Don't yer worry, miss; I'll pertect yer!"

Jack had been exquisitely sensitive to the temptation which Miriam suggested. One stroke for freedom, and all these crudities and absurdities would pass away from them forever! But the roseate atmosphere that surrounded them chilled and darkened a trifle as the impulse knocked at his heart; and the words of the two unconscious mortals made him pause. What would become of them? Had they not the right to live out their earthly lives to the end? Clear perception came to him, also, on the instant, of the greatness of Jim's devotion and self-abnegation. He felt humbled before him!

Miriam perused his mind and saw his answer to her plea. She sighed, and fortified herself to postpone paradise. The thought of her father strengthened her.

"Yes, love, we will not slight God's gift," was her response.

The luminous gold and rose brightened and deepened again, and the delicate filaments were interwoven in a warp and woof of lovely figures, dancing lightly through the aerial fabric, keeping time to the measure of their hearts. They drew nearer.

Contemplating with spiritual sight the scene without, they beheld these bewildered souls groping pitifully in darkness and ignorance, seeking through evil and unknown good. Driven helplessly hither and thither by monstrous spirits of hatred, greed, and terror, they fought and yelled and reeled in blind frenzies, lost to love and sanity.

And yonder loomed Torpeon, a dark shape of wrath and tyranny, like the black twist of a tornado reddened with lightnings. He, too, was driven helpless by accursed powers he knew not, most a slave when he deemed himself most dominant. He struck vengefully to right and left, laughing terribly as his victims tumbled, blasted, at his feet, blind to the souls thus freed who hurtled up unseen to assail him. At times the whole scene assumed the appearance of a writhing mass of poisonous serpents stinging one another to death, and the great serpent in the midst, venom oozing from his bloody jaws, burying his fangs in his own swollen coils. And Jack, an hour since, had longed to add his strength to make this horror yet more horrible! He groaned in humiliation.

"They are our fellow creatures; let us go out and save them!" said Miriam.

"You!" he exclaimed, disturbed. "Remember Torpeon's mark! I will go!"

She smiled into his eyes. "I no longer fear it, or him; and you cannot prevail alone."

Jenny and Jim were absorbed in the excitement of the battle. Neither saw Miriam turn from the window and pass out of the room, apparently alone.

CHAPTER XXX
ZARGA MAKES AMENDS

ZARGA had met her mistress, alone and unseen, immediately after the breaking up of the high court of justice. The place was on the island, at the spot where the pavilion had stood; but the pavilion was gone, and the island was rocky and barren. The change reflected too clearly to be disregarded the alteration which had been wrought in the girl's ambitions and hopes. Lamara was standing beside a thorn-tree. The birds and the Nature people had departed. Zarga approached with lagging steps. A spring, which had formerly been the fountain in the inner court, bubbled up from a cavity in the rock and trickled away along a stony channel toward the sea.

"There is no labor more blessed than to bring back beauty and happiness from banishment, and make them bloom and be fragrant again," Lamara said in a tender voice. "You can do work that will more than make good the mischief; and out of all that might undertake it, I shall entrust it to you."

"You trust me still?" said the girl. "I don't trust myself!"

"We learn self-trust by being trusted by others," Lamara returned. "The welfare of all our people is in your hands. It lies with you, also, to give back happiness to the strangers whom you wronged, and perhaps to save from destruction the planet from which your own ancestors came hither!"

The girl looked frightened and doubtful. "I loved him!" she muttered.

Lamara shook her head. "You were misled by a fantom shaped out of your own vanity and curiosity, by an agent who sought thus to use you for purposes of his own. When your wisdom reawakes you will recognize the trick. Call upon the good and truth that I have always seen in you—I see them now, struggling to be free again!—and you will win a victory that will wipe out your shame and bring you love and honor!"

"What is it I must do?" asked the girl, paling and flushing by turns with the conflict in her heart.

"Your kinsman, Torpeon, applying his deep penetration into the hidden places of nature to ill ends, to satisfy and insane lust for power, has for a long time past used every resource of science to devise a means to unloose the ties that bind his planet to its orbit, and to set out upon a career of universal conquest and dominion. He led himself to believe that he would be able to control its course among other worlds, and to steer it to other systems, and finally to draw in his train such a retinue of subject planets as would empower him to create and control the fate of starry organisms mighty as Orion and the Pleiades.

"His spiritual blindness, which is as great as his insight into material conditions, prevented him from realizing that the laws which hold the stars are only outwardly physical, and that their spiritual causes are beyond human power to originate or modify. Yet power to destroy is given to man; and so far as the first steps of his plan are concerned, he might have succeeded had not agencies been found so humble as not to be suspected which suddenly upset his preparations.

"This reverse took place but yesterday. But Torpeon had reserved a desperate alternative, which he will now seek to put in operations. Rather than surrender to her lawful betrothed husband the woman whom he stole from him, he will violently tear apart his earth, with all its inhabitants, from its moorings, and hurl it headlong and unguided through space to what destiny he cares not; but its speedy annihilation is certain, and may possibly involve others in its ruin. This monstrous crime, unless a power greater than his can avert it, he has the means to perpetrate. That greater power must be wielded by ourselves, and I have chosen you, my trusted and loved companion, to arouse and set it in motion."

Zarga's eyes began to sparkle, her bosom rose, and she lifted her body erect. Lamara, steadfastly observing her, continued:

"You have studied with me the constitution of our realm, and know by what methods we can, by united efforts, achieve results beyond the reach of any individual compass, how exalted soever. Our present task is formidable; perhaps none more arduous could be imposed upon us; and every member of every society on our globe must cooperate in it. To insure this result, I now appoint you, Zarga, my ambassador to our people. No function more honorable is in my power to bestow; for, to discharge it involves energy and faithfulness beyond the limits and development of all but few. Ask your own soul whether you shall accept or decline it! It is an opportunity, not a command."

"Such forgiveness as yours is worthy of the heart that conceived it; I pray the spirit that it may create in me power to fulfil the trust," said Zarga after a pause. "I see in my soul only ashes; but if you can believe that in may bloom again, I will believe it, too. At least I will spend what life I have in the attempt. What am I to say to the people?"

"Tell them that, at the signal of the ring, which will be visible to all at once, each head is to marshal his society in the supreme Saturnian order. The will of all is to be made one will, in harmony with the recorded will of the spirit. Tell them that the strain will be great, but constancy will prevail. Tell them that the hands of the little children are to be laid, above all, upon the uniting cord; for innocence and love hold the universe together. Let this be done, and Tor shall not be unseated from its place."

Lamara spoke with solemn emphasis, lifting up her arms and her face, as if addressing not so much Zarga in person as the divine qualities of helpfulness and devotion which were to be exemplified in her. Zarga knelt before her, and the arms slowly descended with the gesture of benediction. There was an interval of silence, and then the girl arose and turned to begin her long pilgrimage. Lamara gazed thoughtfully after her, and smiled to observe that violets and wood anemones unfolded their petals in the path of her footsteps; a thrush broke into song, and one or two of the small Nature people peeped out timidly from crevices of the rock.

That day there was the sound of a voice traveling over Saturn, from east to west and from south to north. None had heard its like before, but its meaning was comprehended by all; and the messenger, though unseen, was recognized as the emissary of the highest. Men and women, youths and maidens, and little children, lambent in snow-white flames, came forth from their dwellings, and from the shadows of the groves; up from the murmuring watercourses they came, and from the coolness of the moss-draped ravines; they left their works and enjoyments, their meditations and their worshiping; they stood upon the mountain-tops, and gathered upon the seashore, and gazed skyward, listening and mute, while the flying voice passed over them, leaving its words of warning and exhortation behind. The songs of the birds were hushed as it went by, lest their careless music cause the message to be missed; the animals stole into their coverts, and the Nature people scurried in and out of the forest glades and caverns, awed and excited, they knew not why.

As the voice swept on, region after region of the mighty planet, with their multitudinous communities, caught the call to duty, and gathered in their places, to be ranged by their leaders into rhythmical cohorts and battalions, to subdue their myriad impulses into one impulse, to turn their innumerable thoughts into one thought, to communicate through the linked hands and measured footfalls, through long inter-weavings and choral chantings, the gathering strength of one will welded of all wills into a single flawless and irresistible chain.

And still the warning voice swept on, searching out the farthest valleys, arresting the wayfarers across the plains, overtaking the voyagers upon the boundless lakes, pausing not for tropic heats or arctic colds, never pausing or faltering, resolute to bear the tidings to every creature, and to keep faith to the last. Many there were that marveled who the messenger might be, but there was no answer. Zarga's face was veiled; she performed her mission unknown and unsuspected; only her voice announced her. And only her secret heart knew whence came the strength that enabled her to persevere to the very end.

But when the long day was done she found herself among the sublime and icy silences of the virgin north. No creature lived here; no plant grew; enormous snowfields extended in smooth undulations; immemorial glaciers sloped silently from the mountainsides; frozen peaks glittered aloft, pointing to the unmoving stars. She alighted near the mouth of a great ice cavern, very weary but content. The duty laid upon her had been accomplished.

With the last strength remaining to her she crept into the cavern; to her failing eyes it bore a likeness to the chamber in the crystal mountain which her art had adorned for the festival of love, never to be consummated. A dark splendor of colors glowed within, receding into beautiful mysteries of gloom. Zarga dragged herself to the center of the cavern, and lay down, pillowing her golden head on a lump of ice. She might rest, at last!

"It was for him I did it!" she said to herself; "He will live and be happy with her, and I, too, am happy. He will never know that I died for him;

but Lamara will understand, and she and the spirit will forgive me much, because I did my best to make amends."

Her eyes closed, and there was silence, never to be broken.

CHAPTER XXXI
TORPEON

TORPEON now fought single-handed against the maddened thousands of his subjects. He laughed as he fought. He cleared a space around him, and at every wave of his truncheon a man fell. But they still came on, for they were desperate. They knew that, so long as Torpeon survived, misery, torture, and death would be their portion. The gage of battle having been thrown down, there could be no truce or quarter until he was slain; and if he were to be victorious, so much the more reason for them to fight to the death. They hated him more than they loved their own lives. They had served him in fear, and groaned in their servitude. Now the hour had come for liberty or annihilation.

"Snatch his truncheon from him," they shouted to one another. "Tear him to pieces!"

Torpeon smiled, and death leapt out from his hand. But they still drove in upon him, for they were very many, and the fight was to the finish.

A gigantic creature, half ape, hairy and hideous, nurtured in the caverns and gorges of the dark mountains, came toward him from behind, crouching low behind the others, crawling between their legs, his lips drawn back from his grinning fangs, snarling in his throat, gripping in one hand a flint with a jagged edge. The flint had been soaked in the venom of crushed serpents. Asgar, realizing the opportunity, roused those in front to a fiercer attack, so that the prince's attention might be diverted from the true point of danger. He tossed his thick arms frantically, and his gross body shook as he shrieked out his orders. Torpeon caught sight of him over the heads of the nearer fighters; he lifted his staff and pointed it at him. The invisible bolt flew to its mark. With a screech of rage and agony, Asgar sprang in the air and fell dead, the top of his skull blown off and his brains spattering the heads and faces of those behind him.

"Good old Asgar!" said Torpeon, chuckling in his beard. "Who next?"

But, an instant after, there rose from the crowd such a yell of horrible triumph and bloodthirsty frenzy as made the previous uproar seem tame by comparison.

The man-ape, seizing his chance, burst through the foremost ranks of those who hemmed the prince in from the rear, and made his spring. He alighted on Torpeon's back, his short legs gripping him round the body, while his left arm, powerful as a bar of iron, encircled his throat, and with his right hand, armed with the poisoned flint, he strove to dash death into his face. Torpeon, overbalanced by the immense weight of the grisly creature, and half throttled by the squeeze of the hairy arm, staggered back and nearly fell, striving all the while to bring to bear the truncheon; but his antagonist warded it off with his upthrown shoulder; and now a headlong rush by those in front threw the prince off his feet, and he would have fallen had he not been held up by a simultaneous rush by those behind. By a titanic effort of strength he wrenched himself free from the strangler, and, twisting about, laid him dead with his staff; but not before the other, with a final blow of his armed fist, had succeeded in wounding him on the forehead with his envenomed stone.

At that juncture the gates of the castle were thrown open, and Miriam appeared on the threshold. Those who first caught sight of her uttered shrill cries of amazement and alarm, which turned the attention of others from their enemy; and in a moment the whole mob was facing toward her. None of them had ever seen her before, nor any creature resembling her; and the unknown terrified them. Her beauty and dignity struck them as a menace. She could have come for no other reason than to succor Torpeon, and therefore to attack them. They hesitated, wavering back and forth, not knowing with what powers she might be armed, or in what form the new assault would be made. But the masses in the rear, heartened by their advantage over the prince, forced forward those in front, and the space between her and them grew narrower. Miriam, on her side, after casting a comprehensive glance over the tumult, stepped out from the gateway and advanced straight toward the storm-tossed multitude. She seemed alone, for the companion who walked at her side was invisible to their eyes.

Torpeon, meanwhile, had gained a respite; but he was aware of his wound and of the deadly peril it involved. Already he felt the first chill of the poison congealing the current of his blood. For the time being, however, by the use of the charm against such dangers which he possessed, he was able to ward off the effects in some measure; but what aided yet more to restore him was the apparition at such a moment of Miriam.

It kindled a wild fire in him; for he could interpret her presence only as designed to aid him or to share his fate. She loved him, then! At that thought so fierce a tempest of emotions burst out in his heart that he shivered like a tower in earthquake; all else was lost, but she was won, and of what value beside that was any other victory or defeat! He threw himself toward her, slipping in blood, stumbling over corpses; if he could but gain the castle with her, and force his way to that guarded crypt below where was hidden the engine prepared against the last emergency, lurking there like a monstrous jinnee, biding its time to defy God and nature, he could wrench asunder the invisible cables that bound his globe to a hated obedience, and soar with her untrammeled into cosmic freedom. There would be leisure, then, to heal him of his wound; or, if death must come, it would find him in her arms. His brain began to reel; moments of blankness drifted across his mind; but he staggered onward.

To Jack the spirits of the slain were more conspicuous than were the still incarnate, and he perceived that they swarmed round the prince, bewildering his brain, urging him to insane thoughts, causing him to step amiss, and distracting his attention from the assaults of the mob. They constituted a peril more immediate than from the latter. He saw, too, that he could himself exercise more control over these dead than over the living. They saw and feared him, whereas the others divided their menace between Torpeon and Miriam.

The spirit of the hairy monster, reeking from his own corpse, and incomparably more hideous and infuriated than before, was especially active against his slayer. At this instant, seconded by the rampant specter of Asgar, he swerved Torpeon from his course, so that he tripped over Asgar's body and fell headlong. The shock of the fall caused the truncheon to fly from his hand and left him defenseless. The mob made a rush for him.

No wrath or hatred against any living creature dwelt in Jack's soul; his insight had now become too penetrating and comprehensive for that. He had no desire but to save the prince. With a gesture he drove back the murderous ghosts from their prey, but he could influence only indirectly the savage hosts of the earth-bound; and that would not suffice!

Miriam, however, hesitated not a moment. Unarmed and unshielded, she sprang to the rescue. The mob, lacking a leader either dead or living, gave back in transient panic before her, not knowing what magic weapon might be at her command. Torpeon struggled to his feet once more. But he was no longer fully conscious of what he did. Miriam said to Jack:

"Guide him to the castle, where he will be safe; leave these poor creatures to me."

But a new element entered into the fray.

Jim, who had not noticed Miriam's absence from the upper window, where he and Jenny had been observing the conflict below, had been greatly startled to behold her emerge from the gateway, apparently unaccompanied. Whatever had been his original plan of campaign, the turn of affairs had seemed so well calculated to forward his main object, that he had been satisfied to let it continue; a free fight, too, is always a captivating spectacle for a boy. But Miriam's unexpected participation in the battle threatened total disaster to all his projects; and the necessity of protecting her swept all other considerations from his mind.

Disregarding the lamentations of poor Jenny, he seized his crutch and made off incontinently for the stricken field. He had not stopped to consider what form his intervention should take; he thought of himself not at all, except as an instrument of use for persons he loved; but he had full confidence in the efficacy of Solarion's gift.

Selfless love for others is the soul of the faith that works what we regard as miracles. Things may happen in our daily walk and pass unobserved that are in their essence more marvelous than the transformation of a blackthorn stick into a battle-charger.

Be that as it may, it was a mounted cavalier who issued forth from the castle just as Miriam helped the dazed and moribund Prince of Tor to his feet and assigned him to Jack's care while she faced the mob. She faced them, but made no demonstration. They were intimidated, but it would not be for long. The sight of Torpeon making his escape into the castle set fire to their rage anew. They were gathering courage for an onset.

Jim, as he rode forth, marked Torpeon entering in, but he had no consciousness of his guide. He had no misgiving but that his boss was many thousands of miles distant from this debatable ground. And if he could furnish the means of getting him and the woman he loved together, the chief end of his existence, as he saw it, would be achieved. To what else might happen he was royally indifferent.

"De boss an' de missis is de real goods," he told himself complacently; "not'in' else ain't in dere class; de on'y t'ing ails dem is, dey ain't got no caution! Any guy what makes good in de ring has to be wise to side-steppin'; foot-work is de cheese; but dese here folks o' mine, dey rushes in head down an' wide open. De odder guy lands his uppercut, an' ef de time-keeper ain't on de job wid de bell, dey's counted out! Well, I's de timekeeper for dis roun', an' I figgers ter make a reckud!"

As he rode up to Miriam he hailed her cheerfully.

"Here yer are, miss! Las' call ter lunch! Forw'd cyar on yer right! Hop right aboard while de hoppin's good! On'y line what issers free passes ter N'York! Step lively an' avoid de rush! All clear ahead, no sidin's nor interference!" He had dismounted and taken his place on the left, with his hand ready to assist her in mounting. "Put yer foot here, miss, an' up yer goes! Are yer on? Firs' stop, Sattum, an' de boss waitin' fer yer on de platform. So-long!"

"But you must ride behind me, Jim!" said Miriam, holding out a hand to help him to the crupper. The creatures were closing round them.

Jim recoiled with an air of injured dignity. "Say, miss, fer de sake o' Mike, git busy wid yerself! What, me? Is I de sort ter take de boss's place, I arsks yer? Me, I takes me time, see! Jes' you leave dese here slumgullions ter me! Say, cleanin' up a bunch like dat is me middle name! An' I'll lan' in N'York befo' you does, at dat!"

Miriam felt that there was no leisure to parley. She stooped down quickly and caught the little anatomy round the body. But even as she lifted him to the saddle, a heavy stone, hurled with deadly aim and tremendous force, struck the boy just over the heart. He gave a gasp, and lay limp across her saddle-bow. The horse bounded into the air.

A blaze of light, spanning the heavens from east to west, arched across overhead—Lamara's sign of the ring to the Saturnians. The whole stupendous circle had burst into dazzling flame. That appalling splendor sent its rays throughout the firmament. Simultaneously, Miriam saw the solid globe from whose surface she had just risen rock and lurch like a balloon straining at its moorings. It seemed to be endowed with a terrible life; it yawed and plunged this way and that; groanings broke from it; the peaks and crags were overthrown in ruin; the boiling rivers were tossed from their channels and emptied into the belching craters of the volcanoes; and the Bitter Sea, rushing from its bed, poured its flood over the city and its people. It whirled around the castle, deep down in whose rock-quarried crypt the crazed desperado had set in motion the huge wheels of his impious engine. The waters beat upon the walls and towers; they tottered and crumbled, and, whirling as they fell, buried their builder beneath a pyramid of shattered stone.

But, as Miriam still rose aloft, she saw the vast sphere of Saturn outspread beneath her. Upon its surface, revealed in the intense light of the blazing arch, the myriads of the Saturnians performed in concert the evolutions of their mystic rite. They covered the face of the sphere like a network of many colored strands, ceaselessly shifting and reforming in harmonious figures; a living web, through whose threads coursed the single will and impulse to master disorder with order, darkness with light, hate with love. The great globe was clothed with a lovely iridescence, the mingling hues of which united in white shafts of light, bearing in their bosom the invisible rays of spiritual energy which should counteract and overcome the profane forces of dissolution. Slowly but irresistibly the gigantic struggle issued in the victory of law and peace, and the infernal armies of rebellion and chaos gave way before the might of their opponents. Miriam saw the throes and heavings of tortured Tor gradually subside, and the planet resumed the steadfast track of its orbit. The embassy of Zarga, faithfully fulfilled, had not failed of its object.

A hand was at her bridle rein, though invisible to her sight; but she yielded with confidence to its guidance.

"Dearest," she said, "must that draft which you accepted for my sake from Solarion part us on earth henceforth, or may we be fully reunited here?"

"I took the risk, beloved," he replied. "What will be the outcome I cannot tell. We love each other, and love's gains must always be greater than its sacrifices, for any sacrifice in that cause can but give each of us to the other the more. But it seems to me that the halo of which Lamara told me must be the reward of a soul so loyal, loving, and magnanimous as to give all for the sole happiness of giving. No other gift is pure enough to be divine."

Tears gushed to Miriam's eyes; and she bent down and kissed the forehead of the little gnome who lay lifeless across her saddle.

The flames of the ring subsided as they dropped in wide circlings toward Saturn. The choral dance had ceased, and the people had retired to their places. But the planet bloomed with a fresh, unprecedented beauty; the air rang with birdsongs, and was rich with flower-fragrance. When Miriam alighted on the turf in front of the amphitheater, a deputation of the little Nature people were awaiting her. They took Jim's body and laid it on a bier which they had brought, made of green boughs woven together and covered with flowers, and bore it away, to the music of quaint chantings, just as Lamara and some others came up the slope from the sea.

CHAPTER XXXII
DIVIDED

LAMARA took Miriam in her arms and kissed her. The caress revived the girl's drooping strength and sent currents of joyous sunshine rippling through her veins. A glorious light invested Lamara herself, as if from a divine baptism.

"Saturn will bless you forever," Lamara said. "You have brought us a new era. We were relaxed in a dangerous ease, too well content with what we were, and too little mindful that what we receive loses its virtue if it be not passed on to others. Tor was a lesson never to be forgotten. The worst fate was barely averted; and it will be our happy task to create there a state of life less gloomy and cruel than they have known till now. Torpeon is gone; but we pray for his forgiveness; for much of the sin of his transgression lies at our door. Zarga—we hope for her return, but she is long absent."

"Zarga is at peace," said Solarion, who had joined the group unobserved. "The wound she received in the cavern, which she never disclosed, bled inwardly. It could never have been healed in this world. She made amends; and love will find her out."

Miriam gazed hopefully from one to another face of those who surrounded her. But the face her soul longed for was not visible, nor was the sense of his presence any longer felt as before. She had not courage to ask the question that trembled on her lips. But all looked tenderly upon her. Argon, whose cheeks were wet with the tears shed for his sister, took her hand and kissed it. Aunion's eyes dwelt upon her with deep benignity; but there was silence till Solarion addressed her.

"The mystery of life and death is never solved on earth, little sister," he said; "nor can it be known when or why one will be taken and another left. But lovers who know love have believed that what seems parting may be the means of a dearer union; because they found that kisses of mortal lips foretold more than they could fulfill."

"It is not that I would call him back, if he is gone," she replied tremulously, "but that I might follow where he is."

Solarion smiled and said: "It is not far to go."

"But you will return to your home again," added Lamara, putting an arm around her. "Your father has need of you; and Mary Faust would speak with you. You have seen and known things they will be glad to hear. You will find all prepared for your reception. Come, now, and let us spend a farewell hour together."

But Miriam bent her head upon Lamara's bosom and wept.

"I have no strength for more farewells," she said. "I can have faith that there may be happiness for me; but it shines so far away, and the path to it seems so lonely, and I am so weary of journeying, and fear of myself is so heavy upon me, that I wish to be put upon my way at once. If I delayed here, my heart would still seek for my beloved, and I could find no rest.

"I know"—she looked sadly at Solarion—"that, after all is done, I may not find him; but there is comfort in the seeking; to pause and turn aside even among you, friends who are so dear, would breed shadows in me which would throw their darkness over you. Your world is too bright and great for me. My mind cannot compass it; my nature is not formed to its measure; its joys are all too sublime, its thoughts too profound. Had you not—as I feel you have—screened its full splendors from my senses, I could not have endured them.

"God, I think, fashions each of us to fit the world to which we are born, and has made the spaces that separate them so vast as an admonition to us to hold to our own. I can bring to my home people no message wiser than this. They are restless and ambitious and reach out after remote and hidden things; they create wealth and torture Nature to make her reveal her secrets; in their anxiety to miss no gain and lose no pleasure, they hurry to and fro, and perish in pursuit of a fantom whose substance was all the while beside them. I have shared their errors; but among you I have gathered some truth.

"The only knowledge that enriches comes from within; all that is immortally loveable comes to us as spontaneously and simply as the songs of birds and the perfume and colors of flowers. You have taught me much; but he from whom I have learned most is the one whom I had least regarded till near the end; the little being whose only self was his loyalty to others, who made the great voyage from no motive but to serve those he loved; and, when his end was gained, died with a smile on his lips in the act of resigning his last chance of life to insure their safety. Your Nature people have taken his body; I pray God that I may have become worthy, when I die, to be near the place where God keeps his soul!"

Solarion and Lamara exchanged a glance.

"The flowers on Jim's grave," Solarion said, "will draw their perfume and beauty from the pure devotion which the rough rind of his nature concealed. Death discloses the loveliness in him which was disguised while he lived by the veil of his humility. He is a word of the spirit, spoken through the letter of a humble and mutilated body, which being now interpreted, will sweeten and enlighten the world."

"Nevertheless," observed Lamara—and something in her tone caused a secret hope to stir in Miriam's heart—"not every flower owes its bloom and fragrance to a grave!"

With Aunion preceding, the friends now entered the amphitheater, whose august interior was first revealed to Miriam. But it was no longer filled with countless thousands of human creatures, nor did the judges sit upon their thrones. Instead, the enormous crater of the auditorium was thronged from base to summit with roses of all tints; the vines clambered luxuriantly from bench to bench, peeped from every aperture, blushed and blanched from side to side of the sun-steeped bowl, and tossed their joyful faces toward the sky from the topmost parapets. From the fervent gold of their hearts was dispensed an incense that seemed to find its way into the very soul of the beholder and to feed the inmost springs of life with sumptuous delight. The soft yet imperial splendor of each blossom added its gracious potency to its neighbors, till the whole arena palpitated in an apotheosis of the flower-queen—the rapturous triumph of the immortal rose. To breathe was ecstasy; and the eye drank unappeasable drafts of delicate intoxication. As Miriam moved forward, her spirit subdued to a harmonious tranquility, the rich notes of nightingales welled out upon her ear, transmuting by their alchemy the realms of color and perfume into song.

And now, bestowed by what hand she knew not, she felt the clustering of roses on her head; their petals caressed her cheeks; the heavy blooms mantled her shoulders and trailed even to her feet; no bride prepared for her nuptials was ever so attired. She was drawing near to a bower erected in the center of the arena—a structure woven of roses, white as a virgin's soul without, within rose red as the pure passion of her heart. Into that glow she entered, and found a golden altar, before which she knelt and closed her eyes.

Ah, if the bridegroom would come!

CHAPTER XXXIII
JIM'S REWARD

AN East Indian reclining chair, eased with soft pillows and placed in the embrasure of a western window, took the rays of the sinking sun, and was breathed upon by the light evening air. The window was open, and across a breadth of green park enclosure was visible the broad gleam of the Hudson, flowing seaward beneath its parapets of brown rock. Miriam, as she lay in the chair, had just opened her eyes upon this familiar scene; and not less familiar was the spacious room which she knew she could see by turning her head; she had often sat there on summer evenings like this, holding discourse with Mary Faust on matters, deep or trifling, of heaven and earth. There was a wonderful scent of roses in the room, and when she lifted a hand indolently to her head she was surprised to find herself wearing a crown of roses; roses, too, trailed along the sides of the chair and hung down to the floor, as if she were lying upon a bed of them. Magnificent flowers they were, and not of any species that she remembered. Where had they come from?

As she idly debated this question in her mind, she was conscious of a sort of gentle puzzlement in her thoughts; the continuity of events seemed broken; she could not recall what had preceded her coming to this room. Had she fallen asleep, and had Mary caused her to be conveyed hither in that condition? She was not wont to take naps at this hour. Had she been ill? That seemed still more unlikely; illness and she were strangers. Had Mary, for some undisclosed purpose, thrown her into a trance? Least probable of all!

What had they been doing that day? She had arrived early; she had found Mary absorbed in mathematical calculations of the transcendent order; they had exchanged a few words, and then Miriam had gone alone into the laboratory. There she had paced up and down for a while, revolving the great enterprise which they had so long been working on together. Would it, after all, prove actually practicable? Theoretically, there seemed to be no opening for doubt; and yet— Finally, the better to pursue her meditations, she remembered seating herself in the chair of the psycho-physical engine; and her hand—her right hand—had rested on the head of the great lever. Would anything really happen were she to press it down?

She recalled the flitting of that thought through her brain. The lever was so nicely adjusted as to move at a very slight impulse; and then—

She uttered a sharp cry—a cry of terror. She huddled down in the chair, half raising her hands as if to ward off a blow. She panted as from a race. Her feeling was that a world was falling down upon her to crush her. After a few moments she pressed her hands over her eyes and quick moans broke from her. She felt a hand laid gently on her head—a cool, soothing hand. By and by she sat up and stared fearfully about her.

"Oh, Mary, what happened?" she muttered. "Was it true?"

"Take your time, dear," Mary replied. "You got back safe. It's all right. Shall I tell Jenny to bring you a cup of tea?"

"Jenny! But she was—we were taken up in a moment. Oh, my poor Jenny!"

"Jenny was my affair," said Mary Faust, with her grave smile. "I furnished her, and of course I provided for her return. She is none the worse for the trip."

Miriam had not yet recovered her spiritual footing. "Saturn!" she murmured. "Lamara—Zarga! Torpeon!"

Suddenly she snatched at the right sleeve of her dress, and tore it across, exposing the shoulder. She scrutinized it eagerly. The mark was still there, but instead of red it now appeared as a white scar. Mary Faust eyed it with interest.

"He must have stamped it deep!" she observed. "It has survived your Saturnian incarnation. But its power is gone; it's only a memento now."

"I was there!" said Miriam wonderingly; "and this is our own earth again!"

"It was a trying experience," said her friend in a matter-of-fact tone; "but our science is vindicated, and we need never repeat the experiment. We'll talk it over at our leisure some other time. What lovely roses you brought back with you! The place looked like a conservatory! We understand the principle, of course; but it was exquisitely done! I wish I could have been with you; but I kept in touch as well as I could."

"They know and honor you there; and Solarion!"

"Yes, I have much to thank him for. But don't be agitated, dear; things will take their proper places by degrees. The world will be under a great obligation to you. Your departure was a little premature, but after all it was better so. There was only one sad thing about it; and that, too, has beauty and consolation. Dear little Jim!"

Miriam turned and bent upon her friend a long and poignant look. She tried to command herself, but her lips quivered and tears ran down her face.

"So may worlds," she faltered, "and death in all of them! Jim was a hero, and he died for me; but why must the other be taken, and I be left? Without him, what use am I? I had begun to know what love is; and now I am alone! Mary, his spirit was with me in that last terrible scene; I could even see him and hear his voice. Why couldn't he stay with me, if only as a spirit? God has all power, in heaven and on earth!"

"The scope of science does not include such problems," said Mary Faust composedly. "But I should suppose that any conscious intercourse between the two planes of life must be exceptional and transient—in our present stage of development, at any rate. Spirit consorts with spirit, and flesh with flesh; that is normal and wholesome. To overstep the boundaries is dangerous and leads to confusions. Neither side can be of use in its place if it is continually trespassing upon the other. If I had a lover, and knew that he was still alive and loved me, why should I mourn because his senses and mine function for a while under different conditions, and are themselves of a different order? If he had ceased to be, or loved me no more, that might be a cause for mourning."

"You are wise and reasonable," said Miriam, with a sigh; "but it seems to me to be cause for mourning, too, that a warm, loving, beating human heart must survive in the ice of your logic, with only a memory and a hope—which may become frozen, too."

"Matters may turn out better than you think," was Mary Faust's reply. "Meanwhile, your father is waiting in the next room. Will you go to him?"

"Dearest father!" exclaimed Miriam rising. "Yes, there are more loves than one."

She wiped the tears from her cheeks, and with the rose-wreaths still clinging about her, followed her friend into the shadowy spaces of the laboratory.

From the gloom the sturdy figure of the white-headed old contractor started forward, grasped his daughter by the shoulders with trembling hands, and gazed into her face with a devouring look.

"Me own colleen!" he cried in a breaking voice. "Come back safe and alive to her old daddy! Glory be to God and all the blessed saints! Oh, honey, honey, don't ye never be doin' the likes again. Sure, the heart was most bruck in me!" He held her to him with an almost desperate clutch. "Take all ye want in this world—marry any man ye like—but, stay where the old daddy that loves ye can feast his eyes on ye."

"Darling daddy!" murmured she; "You're all I have left; thank God for you."

"Long live Oireland!" rejoined the old man fervently but incoherently.

Two tall figures stood in the background; one of them began to come forward, not quickly, but with an inevitableness like the drawing of planet to planet. The other, with a cigar between his fingers, watched the scene with an amused but genuine interest.

Miriam did not observe the newcomer till he was close upon her. Without directly looking at him, she involuntarily drew back a little, with a feeling that no outsider should intrude upon this meeting. At this moment Mary Faust touched a button, and the room was filled with light.

Miriam's arms fell to her sides, nor was there strength in her to lift a finger. Nor had her lips power to form themselves into a smile; but the soul within her rushed into her widely opened eyes with such a radiance of speechless joy that the others turned aside and retired noiselessly into a remote part of the great chamber, realizing that the place of these two was holy ground. He came forward another step; but not yet did she believe that this was more than a return of that blessed vision which had been granted her on the other side of space. Oh, was not this happiness enough!

She seemed to herself to be floating in a shining void of heaven, with the glow of a great warmth suffusing her. How real, how near seemed his face. Or was it that she herself had unawares been borne to paradise, and they were met to part no more!

"I cannot bear it, love!" she whispered. "It seems too real. And then to have you go again."

But now she felt a touch; his arms, firm and strong, were round her;

his lips were upon her lips, and no illusion or magic prevented them. Her cry sprang forth like the warbling of a bird—joy, passion, and music in one:

"Oh, Jack; my darling, my love, my own! It's you; it's you, you, your own blessed self! Jack, it's forever!" Her hands caught at him, gripped him hard, his arms, his shoulders, his face; her fingers plunged in his hair. "Oh, love, you were dead, and are alive again!"

Twilight had entered into night when the lovers compelled themselves to issue from their paradise, and join the others where they sat at a table near an open window in the laboratory. The window was wide and high, and commanded a large view of the heavens in that quarter. A great star hung midway aloft, giving out a serene light. The lights in the room had been lowered, as if not to detract from its radiance. Miriam's hold upon her lover's arm tightened:

"Jack, we were there"

"Eight hundred million miles!" said he.

"And you went there for me!"

"I would go to Sirius for you; the universe is not large enough to keep me from you. Nothing is too far for love."

The tall man who had been Jack's companion rose from the table, and came forward with a jolly bow and smile. Miriam recognized Sam Paladin.

"I'm very glad to see you home again, Miss Mayne," he said, grasping her hand. "I used to fancy I'd done some trotting about, but I shall sit at your feet henceforth. As for that boy Jack, he deserves less credit. Who wouldn't do as much for such an object?"

"Sure and I'd have gone meself, if they'd let me," said Terence Mayne.

Jenny brought the tea, curtsying happily to her mistress and looking more natural than ever.

After some chat about some business and politics, chiefly between Terence and Sam, Mary Faust suddenly excused herself and went out. She returned after a few minutes.

"I have had a message from our friends," she said, addressing Miriam and Jack more especially, and with as much simplicity as if the message were from down-town. "Lamara and the judges have conferred, and she wishes you to know the result. Will you follow me—all of you?"

They got up, and she led them to a part of the laboratory partitioned off from the main room, and fitted up somewhat after the manner of an oratory. Neither the lovers nor the other two had any notion of what was to happen.

There was an oval window looking to the south and east, through which the rays of the planet Saturn fell and rested upon a couch, draped with a robe of white samite, bordered with blue. Mary Faust, with a reverent gesture, turned back this coverlet, and the body of Jim was revealed, with his crutch beside him. There was no other illumination in the place than what proceeded from the planet: but as the eyes of the spectators grew accustomed to the dimness, the face of the little gnome was distinctly visible. There was a trace of the good-humored grin on his lips, with which he had met all the vagaries of fortune; but also an innocent lovableness which his indomitable spirit had disguised during his earthly life. All gazed upon this spectacle with affectionate sympathy.

"Lamara told me," said Mary Faust, breaking the silence, "that the highest honor among Saturnians is indicated by a halo, symbolizing the perfect love that has no thought of self. It is bestowed by the ruler of the planet, sitting in counsel with the wisest of the realm; but the gift does not come from them, but from the Source of life and love, who communicates it to them as almoners. And she asked me to bring you here for witness."

As they stood about the couch, Miriam's hand in Jack's, Sam and Terence gravely attentive, the faint, diffused light gathered more definitely upon the dead urchin's head. At length it seemed as if the light emanated therefrom, rather than from the distant globe. Still it brightened, and now assumed the form of a ring of purest radiance, shining above his forehead; if a circle of pearls could be fire, they would appear thus. It was visible for several minutes; and whether it then vanished, or whether the eyes of the onlookers were unable any longer to discern it, was doubtful. Perhaps it was a thing which only persons of good will and pure heats could have seen at all.

They went out in silence; but the meaning of the halo sank deep into the lovers' souls, and its light guided their life.

CPSIA information can be obtained
at www.ICGtesting.com
Printed in the USA
BVHW070904110821
614085BV00003B/252